Cursing Fate

THE FATED SERIES

Cursing Fate

THE FATED SERIES

Brenda Drake

Entangled Publishing, LLC
2614 South Timberline Road
Suite 109
Fort Collins, CO 80525
Visit our website at www.entangledpublishing.com.

Crave is an imprint of Entangled Publishing, LLC.

Edited by Liz Pelletier
Cover design by Syd Gill
Cover art from Shutterstock

Manufactured in the United States of America

First Edition November 2016

For all the sisters,
And for Paula, who is mine

Chapter One

Having any sort of control seemed elusive lately. Iris Layne fidgeted next to her science project, her eyes firmly set on one person in a cafeteria jam-packed with students, teachers, and parents. Three-dimensional boards, colorful and full of information, kept blocking her view of him as he shuffled among the displays, inspecting the projects.

The cafeteria was hot and muggy.

Iris unscrewed the top to her water bottle and took a long swig, catching another glimpse of him between two tables. His shoulder-length dark hair was pulled back in a man bun. He wore one only after he'd just gotten off his motorcycle, his hair messy from the helmet.

Wade Diaz looked like a typical bad boy, complete with leather jacket and ripped jeans, but she knew the real him. His softer side. They'd known each other since eighth grade when he was scrawny and annoying, but he'd grown up nicely in the last two years. She bit her lip. Would he avoid coming by her display? He'd been dodging her ever since school started several weeks ago. And she hadn't seen him all summer.

They were friends most of ninth and tenth grade, slowly growing into more than friends junior year. When they'd finally gotten together, Iris abruptly ended things and went back to her jerk of an ex-boyfriend. No wonder Wade hated her. But she couldn't stop missing him. He was her best friend. The one she could always count on. If only she could tell him what really happened.

"Hey." Carys startled Iris, and she flinched. "Sorry, didn't mean to scare you." She glanced over her shoulder to where Iris couldn't quite look away. "I wish the two of you would make up already."

Not likely.

Iris had glimpsed him once over summer break during the Fourth of July celebration on the Ocean City boardwalk. After spotting her, he'd abruptly turned and got lost in the crowd. Add that he'd ignored all her texts and calls, even unfriended her on his social media accounts, and she doubted they would ever make up.

Iris gave Carys a slight smile. "Me, too."

"It isn't right that he looks better than me in a bun," she said, scrunching the ends of her dark shoulder-length hair. "I don't know how you gave him up for that."

Iris glanced at her, then to where she was looking. Her heart skidded to a stop. Josh, aka ex-boyfriend, led his pack of idiots down the aisle. Ever since Iris broke things off with him, he'd been a creep. Her once-popular status had plummeted, and now Marsha Simmons was the new queen of the school and Iris had become an outcast.

"Just ignore them," Carys said, pulling a dollar out of her pocket. "Why don't you get me a bottled water? I'll watch your display until they're gone."

"Thanks. You're the best." Iris took the money and made

her way through the maze of projects, stopping at the vending machines.

Iris didn't deserve Carys as a friend. She'd been horrible to Carys. Ditching her to hang out with Josh all the time. Despite all the things she'd done, Carys was the first to forgive Iris. Over summer, they'd grown closer in their friendship.

The doors were propped open by kickstands at the bottom, letting in the smell of fresh-cut grass from the football fields. The light breeze felt good against her sweaty skin. Maryland was beautiful in the fall with the leaves on the trees changing from green to vibrant reds, oranges, and yellows. Soon the pumpkin patch would open, and it would be strange not going with Wade. It was one of their many yearly rituals.

She flattened out the wrinkled dollar before feeding it into the money slot. The machine whirled before rejecting it. She straightened the corners and tried it again. It slid back out.

Someone held a crisp new dollar in front of her face.

"Try this one." Wade's voice sent her stomach to swirling.

Iris turned to face him. "Hey." She didn't know what to say, the speech she'd memorized for if he ever spoke to her again forgotten. His deep brown eyes made all ability to think difficult.

When she hadn't taken the dollar from him, he inserted it into the machine. "What did you want?"

"Um…a water," she said.

He pushed the button, and a bottle thumped into the retrieval bin. She bent to grab it at the same time as he did, touching hands, a spark passing between them.

"Oh," Iris said, straightening. Panic fluttered in her chest. It was silly, but ever since Aster, her older sister, revealed her gift, Iris feared even the littlest static charge.

With a simple touch of a tarot card, Aster could change someone's fate. Usually a bad one. The problem was, she could transfer it to anyone she came into contact with, and a shock would pass between Aster and her victim.

Relax already. Aster isn't here. Iris took in a calming breath.

Wade retrieved the water and raised a curious brow at her. "You okay?"

Iris laughed. It was a soft, nervous one and by the look on Wade's face, he'd noticed. "I'm fine," she said, not sure it was convincing.

"There's a lot of friction in here." He winked. The fact that his comment meant more than just the static between them hadn't escaped her. It was clever how he tied it to their uneasiness toward each other.

He held out the water bottle to her. She reached for it, their hands touching briefly again before he let go, sending her stomach into a nervous flurry again. Why did he always do that to her? It used to be comfortable around him. She could tell him anything and not worry that he'd think she was lame. But things had changed.

They had changed.

When she hadn't spoken, he nodded at the bottle and asked, "That's what you wanted, wasn't it?"

"Yes. Th-Thank you." The tremble in her voice annoyed her.

He gave her one of his killer smiles. The one that tilted slightly and exposed his perfectly aligned teeth. He could be the model in a Crest commercial with that one.

There was a sadness in his eyes that matched how she felt. The night he had come to her house after she ended it with him, just before her Sweet Sixteen birthday party, played like a nightmare in her mind. He had looked tortured—eyes rimmed red. He'd begged her to rethink her decision to get back with Josh. Told her that Josh was a loser and he'd hurt her again. And he was right. Josh had destroyed her.

"I should go," he said. "I'm meeting someone. We'll stop by and check out your project later."

"Okay," was all she could manage to say. Jealousy surged through her. *Are you meeting a girl?* It wasn't her business. She'd had her chance.

As he walked away, all the words she'd wanted to say came to her. *I'm sorry, Wade, for breaking your heart and for getting back with Josh. But it was out of my control. My stupid sister changed our fate. Can we start over? I so wish we could. I miss you.*

She wished she had Aster's ability. Then she could fix things. Gram and Mom had a tarot reader on the boardwalk, Miri, test Iris along with her twin, Violet, to see if they carried the gene. Both came up negative.

They weren't sure if her younger sister, Daisy, carried it. She'd been too freaked out to touch tarot cards after all the crazy stuff that had happened with Aster shifting them. Death, sickness, and messed-up love lives had been the result. But everything worked out, and Aster was off at MIT with her boyfriend, Reese, studying physics.

Except the damage done by changing Iris's and Violet's fates had remained. Violet suffered bullying courtesy of Josh and his friends. And Iris had lost Wade.

And she had lost her friends after her big blowup with Josh. He was the star of the basketball team. His friends had become hers. When they had broken up, their group all sided with him.

She caught a final glimpse of Wade before he disappeared behind the displays. He was staggeringly gorgeous in tight jeans and Doc Martens with those wide shoulders and toned body. Her heart squeezed with so much disappointment and regret, she could hardly breathe.

With a sigh, Iris shuffled around people through the makeshift aisles back to her project and to Carys. Josh Adams and his squad were only a few tables down from hers. With his perfectly styled hair and his steely blue eyes, he was perfect—too perfect—the fantasy of every high school girl with a pulse. Clutching his arm, Marsha Simmons flicked one big blond curl over her shoulder. She'd won the boyfriend lottery, and she wanted everyone to know. Her laughs at his jokes about other students' works echoed through the cafeteria.

Josh was confident on the outside, but inside, he was a boy in pain. He had suffered horrible abuse from his father. It was so bad that Mr. Adams had been arrested three years ago for doing something Josh refused to tell her. No one at school knew about it. He hid it well, except from Iris. Everyone believed his parents were divorced and his father had moved to Seattle for business.

Had Josh told Marsha about his past? Iris had held Josh many times when he'd been upset after therapy sessions. He was such a mess, and she felt the need to fix him. It was probably the reason it took her so long to realize he was a bully.

Stalking the two lovebirds were Perry, Matt, and Iris's ex–best friend, Lauren. Perry was tall and skinny like a pole—he made a perfect center for the basketball team. Matt played point guard. He was shorter and stockier than his friend was. Lauren, a cheerleader, wore her makeup too light for her dark skin, which made it look ashy. She had been Iris's first friend, before Wade, when her family moved in with Gram.

It made her sick to think she had been a part of their circle. Sucked into the thrill of being in the popular crowd. Thrilled to be Josh's girlfriend. His pain causing her to overlook the mistreating of others. It was Wade who had snapped her out of it, reminding her of who she really was. He'd showed her she wasn't the awful person she'd become with Josh. That she could be better. Be strong on her own.

Iris was so distracted watching them, her hip bumped into

a table with a complicated-looking science project on it that had all sorts of gadgets and metal wheels.

"Watch it," a girl peeking through long, blue bangs said. Her name was Jenna or something. A victim of Josh and his group's bullying. She was thin, smart, and a bit awkward. All things that put a target on her back. And Iris should have helped her but hadn't.

"Sorry," Iris said and rushed off, not able to look the girl in the eyes. She stopped. *This has to stop. Swallow your fear, Iris.* But it terrified her to think of how Jenna, or whatever her name was, would react to it.

Iris turned and marched back to the girl. "Hey, Jenna?"

The girl pulled aside her bangs to look at Iris. "It's Johanna," she said and lowered her eyes.

"That's right," Iris said. "Sorry. Um…I've been meaning to tell you—"

Damn this is hard. Okay, you can do this. Just say it already. Iris rubbed her nose. *Why is this so difficult to say?*

Johanna glanced up at Iris, then around the cafeteria, obviously feeling as awkward as Iris.

"Listen," Iris finally said. "I'm sorry for not stopping Josh and the others when they were bullying you. I should have done something."

"You were always nice to me." The corners of Johanna's lips twisted up slightly. "I've stood aside when others have been bullied by them. It's a survival thing. I get it."

"Well, if you ever need anything, let me know." Iris wasn't sure what to do. Should she say anything else? Go in for a hug?

"Thanks. I will." Johanna pretended to adjust something on her project, releasing Iris of her dilemma.

"Okay, so I'll see you around," Iris said and shuffled off to her project.

"How come they're not at their stations?" Carys said

when Iris arrived back at her table.

Iris shot a glance in the direction Carys was looking. *Josh. I came back too soon. Could this night get any better?*

"They were at the beginning," Iris said, handing Carys the water bottle. "The judges must've already seen their work."

Josh's blond hair was shorter than usual and he wore that dark blue shirt he loved so much because it matched the color of his eyes. He had his letterman's jacket on regardless of how hot it was in the cafeteria. *Such a show-off.*

Lauren fell a few steps behind her boyfriend, Perry. Her dark eyes were sympathetic, but she'd never stand up for Iris. Doing so would get her the same outsider status as Iris. In a way, she felt sorry for the other girl. To fit in, Lauren worked tirelessly, straightening her naturally curly hair and painting her face each morning to pass Marsha's approval.

Iris had been the same way. No matter how hard she tried to reach Marsha's standards, it was never good enough. Marsha would point out that Iris's eye shadow was the wrong color or that her hair was too oily. It really gave Iris a complex.

She was about to excuse herself to go to the restroom when Josh spotted her. *Dammit. He's not chasing me off.*

As the group approached, Carys spun to face Iris's project, pulling Iris around with her. "Yours is the most artistic one here. The universe you painted looks three-dimensional."

Iris gave Carys a confused look.

"Pretend you didn't see them," she said through tight lips. "Ignore them."

Iris had broken up quietly with Josh over the weekend, not wanting it to happen during school. But instead, he'd spread it across all his social media sites that he was the one who broke up with her. Called her names and said she had cheated on him. Iris just wanted it all to go away.

That horrible laugh of Marsha's sounded behind Iris. "How lame. It looks more like an art project than a science one."

"Don't give her a hard time," Josh said. For a brief second, Iris was pleased that he'd defended her. But then he added, "She's not that smart. Art is the only subject she's good at."

His words made her insides collapse.

"Yeah," said Perry. "Her twin got all the brains."

The chuckles from his group scratched down her spine, and Iris fisted her hands.

Before she could turn around, Carys grabbed her wrist. "Don't feed the animals," she whispered.

Their group continued down the row, snickering and whispering to one another. Iris shifted to watch them, spotting Wade across the aisle from her. He glared at Josh and his delinquents' retreating backs. When Wade's gaze found hers, the scowl left his face. There was something like concern in his eyes, or maybe pity.

Whatever it was, it made a sudden ache hit her heart, and she couldn't breathe. Couldn't look at him. All the regret and longing burned her eyes. She spun back around and stared at her project, grasping onto the edge of the table to center herself and keep from losing it in front of a cafeteria full of judging eyes.

The words perfectly aligned at the top of her project read, *Composition of a Comet's Tail Using Spectroscopy*. Her eyes followed the brushstrokes of varying blue, yellow, and white hues against a black background. She couldn't understand why they had laughed at her presentation. She'd worked on it for a month with Carys, meticulously painting a comet, its tail trailing behind it as it passed in front of the sun. All the data on the cards, neatly glued off to the side, had passed Carys's scrutiny.

The air adjusted behind her and she stiffened.

Wade?

She slowly turned.

He just stood there, rubbing his chin and studying her project. It was as if an artist tirelessly worked to sculpt his perfect face—sharply angled at all the right places and perfectly rounded at others. Iris realized she was holding her breath, and when she finally remembered to breathe, it came out in a heavy sigh.

Wade raised an eyebrow at her. "You okay?"

Why does he keep asking me that? Do I look like a mess?

"Yes." She could hardly get out the simple word. Why was he here? Whenever he was around, she couldn't think right. Seeing him so much today would definitely cause her to dream about him later. She'd worked hard to rid her mind of the images of her and Wade together. Ones where Wade held her tight and kissed her so deeply it felt like she was that comet on her project, shooting through space so close to the sun she was sure she'd incinerate.

What does he want?

There was a familiar look on his face. One she knew well. He would press his lips together, focusing on anything but her face when he was gathering up courage to ask her something. Just as he was right then.

She swallowed hard. *Is he finally going to forgive me?*

Chapter Two

WADE

Damn. Iris looked hot in her short orange skirt and cropped jean jacket. Wade fought the urge to remove that strand of her strawberry-blond hair always sticking to the right corner of her lips. He knew it was a dumbass move coming over. Running into her at the vending machine should have been enough torture for one day.

Wade cleared his throat. What he wanted to clear was all thoughts of those lips of hers and the memories of their kisses. "The tail's all wrong," he finally said.

"What?" Her eyebrows pinched together, confusion shadowing her face. She rotated away from him and scrutinized her work.

His eyes traveled down her, stopping at the familiar mole on the back of her leg just below the hem of her skirt.

"How's it wrong?" she asked.

His gaze went back to her project. "The comet is passing across the sun. The tail shouldn't be following the comet." He pointed at it. "It should be directed away from the sun, and the dust tail curves toward the orbital path." He air-traced the correct path with his finger over the painting.

"Oh no, what if the judges notice?" Panic sounded in her voice.

Carys placed her hand on Iris's arm. "The judges probably won't notice."

Wade heaved a sigh. "The judges are hardasses this year. One came all the way down from the science lab in Frederick. Do you have a black marker?"

"I think so," Iris said. "Why?"

"Just get it." Though he shouldn't care if Iris suffered—hell, she'd caused him enough pain—he knew she needed a perfect grade on her project. Dena had told him she was almost failing science.

His heart pounded hard in his chest as she held down the hem of her skirt and knelt in front of an overly large canvas bag on the floor. The fabric wrapped tight around her ass. Man, was she sexy. She rifled around inside the tote, her hair falling forward, concealing her face from his view. After finding the marker, she straightened and handed it to him. The touch of her fingers against his hand sent heat and awareness through his body. They locked gazes for several seconds.

"You two should really just get back together." Carys pointed out the white elephant in the cafeteria. "You guys make such a cute couple."

Iris swiftly withdrew her hand and gave Carys a warning glare.

Unlikely. Wade wasn't sure he'd ever be able to trust Iris again. Not since she used him to get back her ex-boyfriend. He snapped the cap off the marker and stepped up to the poster.

"What are you going to do with it?" Iris asked, the definite panic in her voice back.

He ignored her, dragging the black tip across the edge of the comet tail. He darkened it until the dust tail was curved and directed away from the sun. Returning the cap, he stepped back and surveyed his work. "Not perfect. But it'll do."

"You can tell it's been fixed," Iris said.

Carys tilted her head, eyes scanning the board. "Actually, it's not that bad. Besides, they're not judging the art. It's the science that matters."

Iris snatched the marker from Wade's hand. "I can make it better."

Wade took it back from her. She grasped for it, and he pulled it out of her reach.

"The judges are almost here," he said. "You don't want them to see you fixing it."

Her eyes darted to the approaching group—two men and a woman with clipboards. She lowered her hand, giving him a frown before smoothing down her skirt.

The judges stopped in front of her display. Carys gave Iris a silent wave and rushed off to her own table. Iris wringed her hands as the judges examined her science project. Wade stepped back and chuckled under his breath. Her face scrunched with worry and hope was cute. Something like regret sank to his stomach. He missed her. Missed touching her. Missed just hanging out together.

"What's up? I've been looking all over for you," Dena Lee said, coming up to his side. She looked like a boy standing next to him—just shy of average height, her dark hair cropped short.

He glanced at her. "Is that my shirt?"

She wore shiny gray jeans and an unbuttoned black vest over Wade's white T-shirt.

"Yep. I'm running out of options with my wardrobe." She adjusted her weight from one foot to the other. "My mom hasn't caught up to my new style. She keeps buying girly shit."

"It's too big on you." Wade returned his gaze to Iris. She was answering the judges' questions, her hands now free from torture and resting at her sides.

"I'm going to have my grandmother alter it." Dena ran her hand over the expression on the front of the T-shirt: *I'm sqrt[1 + tan2 (c)] and I know it.* "You're just jealous it looks better on me."

Wade chuckled. "Do you even know what it means?"

She paused, feeling herself up. "Um…yeah, something about knowing math. Am I right?"

"You're way off." Wade shook his head. "It's a trigonometric expression simplified to *sec (C)*. So, therefore, it means *I'm sexy and I know it.*"

She snorted. "That's a good one. And it's why this shirt is more suited for me."

Wade laughed and returned his stare to Iris. Her eyes found his and she grinned. She'd changed since Josh's group had shunned her. There was a new vulnerability behind her smiles and a warmth in her eyes. It was hypnotizing, and he could watch her all day, but he wondered how long it would last.

She was fickle—going from Josh to Wade and then back to Josh. It was like he'd suffered whiplash. Their relationship lit up and died faster than a spark off a burning log. But while it lasted, it was better than any relationship he'd ever had. It took several months to get over their breakup.

"Dude, let's get out of here," Dena said. "You're only torturing yourself being around her. And she looks too much like Violet, so you're torturing me, too."

"How is Violet doing?" Wade asked.

Dena shrugged a shoulder. "Okay, I guess. Ever since the whole Violet-and-Dena-making out-gate, she's been distant. Afraid, I guess I'm her first girlfriend. She doesn't have the experience that I have with it all. You know…"

Wade did know. She couldn't shut up about it. Where Wade suffered in private, she would torture any poor sucker who'd listen. Other than her relationship issues, Dena was pretty cool to hang with. She challenged him in chess and could beat anyone in a game of beer pong.

But there was more to them than their affinity for games. They would talk for hours about world issues and they had each other's backs. Dena had filled the gaping hole when he and Iris screwed things up by stepping over the friendship line.

The judges shuffled off to the next table, scribbling notes on the cards attached to their clipboards. Iris took a step forward as if she wanted to stop them, convince them to give her a good grade.

Dena leaned closer to Wade. "If we stand here any longer, just staring, we'll look like creepers."

Wade nodded, giving Iris one last look before shuffling off in the same direction as the judges, passing as close as he could to get a glimpse of their score sheets. The marks were high. Wade turned, giving Iris a thumbs-up.

Iris's shoulders relaxed, and she expelled a relieved breath. She crinkled her nose at him before smiling brightly, and his heart nosedived. Everything she did was adorable.

Dena bumped into his shoulder. "God. You've got it worse than me."

"Shut up," Wade said and walked off. The thing was, he did have it bad. He rounded the corner and continued to the next row, spotting Josh and his groupies. Every time he saw Josh, it reminded him of Iris ditching him for the douchebag. That betrayal stung worse than being kicked in the balls.

Josh and his worshippers were harassing a skinny freshman. Wade had made it his mission to protect the weaker population at Stephen Decatur High School. He didn't have to do much—only walk over and stand by the freshman. Wade patted the guy's back and he flinched. Dena was nowhere in sight. Something must have distracted her on the other row.

"How's it going?" Wade gave Josh a glare. "You messing with my friend here?"

Of course, Josh wouldn't back down; he had his reputation to protect. But he wouldn't do anything, either. Not since he'd lost a fight with Wade a few days before school ended last June.

The jerk was spreading rumors about Iris, and Wade had lost it, leaving Josh with a broken nose and two black eyes.

It made Wade sick to think of Josh doing whatever he did with Iris. And his mind went too far most times. He imagined they'd gone all the way. After all, he once found them at a party in one of the bedrooms. Josh had his hands up Iris's skirt. She was drunk. Wade pulled Josh off her and dragged him outside. If Dena hadn't stopped Wade, it was a good bet he would have killed Josh.

"Come on," Josh said, slouching off. "I'm hungry. Let's ditch this stink hole."

Yeah, run off, shithead.

When the group was a safe distance away, the boy turned to Wade. "Th-thank y-you." Wade remembered the boy from his biology class. Tim. That was his name.

"No problem, bro." Wade patted his back again. "You come to me if they give you any more trouble."

Dena rushed up with Iris trailing her. "Dude, that was classic. You scared him off."

What is she up to? I swear, if she's trying to get Iris and me back together, I'm going to puncture her bike tires.

Wade looked over Dena's shoulder at Iris. Whenever she smiled at him like that, his insides turned to mush. He hated that she had that power over him. But he really hated that it took less than three weeks to destroy their friendship.

"Sorry." Dena shrugged. "She said she had to talk to you."

"It's okay," Wade said.

"Hi." Iris's voice was low and uncertain. "I have a favor to ask you…well, it's more like a job."

Wade waited for her to ask.

She waited for him to say it was okay to ask.

Their eyes were stuck on each other, neither one making a move. Maybe it was because he knew that once she'd asked, he would have to answer, and then she'd be gone. And he would go back to missing her.

Dena sighed. "Just ask him."

She stared at the marker in her hand. "I heard you were trying to raise money. To fix your dad's sailboat. Um…" She glanced up at him with that pleading look he could never resist. "Well," she said. "I need a tutor for science, and I was wondering if I could pay you to do it."

Wade gave Dena a WTF look.

Dena grinned. "What? She asked. I can't lie to her. She's going to be my sister-in-law one day. Besides, you need cash. There's no way you can get it from your mom. She'd lock you up just for stepping on that boat let alone sailing it."

It was no secret. *I do need money*.

He was about to cave. "No. I can't," he said.

"Won't you at least think about it?"

He glanced at Iris. She was biting her bottom lip. A move that made him want to wrap his arms around her, press against her body, and nibble that lip. Heat rose inside him at the thought. *Shit. She does this to me every time.* But he did need the money. He could keep it strictly business.

"Okay," he finally said, and she rewarded him with a smile. "When do you want to start?" He liked how she was wearing her long, strawberry-blond hair lately, a natural wave instead of the straight look she used to have.

"As soon as you can," Iris said. "I have a test next week."

He grabbed the back of his neck, glancing over at Dena.

"Don't look at me. I don't know your schedule."

Wade expelled a breath. "All right. How about tomorrow after school?"

She squealed a little under her breath. "That's perfect. My house?"

"Yeah," he said. "My mom's been crazy with the campaign. She's always working, even when she's home."

"Okay, see you then." She spun on her heel and glided off. He watched her until she disappeared around the row of projects. Her hips moved like a slow-swaying boat.

Dena punched his arm. "Wade? Did you hear me?"

"What?" He pulled his stare away from where Iris once was.

"You two just need to have hot makeup sex or something. The tension between you guys is intense."

"We've never done it," Wade said, heading for the exit.

"Really?" Dena was trying to stay up with Wade's long stride. "Why not?"

"She wasn't ready." He shrugged. "I didn't want to rush her."

"Now that is so sweet." Dena elbowed his side. "You obviously like her. Why not just give it another try?"

"I can't trust her."

They reached the door and Wade gave one last look over his shoulder, his eyes searching until he caught a glimpse of Iris between the displays. *Way to torture yourself, Diaz.* He yanked open the door and waited for Dena to pass through before he let it slam shut behind them.

How the hell was he going to make it through tutoring Iris?

Chapter Three

A brisk wind flapped Iris's jacket as she slammed the Bug's door. Before leaving for college, Aster had given Iris the Volkswagen Beetle. It was Aster's way of apologizing for messing up Iris's life. It helped. Some.

Iris bounded up the steps and pushed open the back door to the large, two-story beach house, a few early fall leaves following her inside. The sweet smell of Gram's baking hit her nose and she inhaled deeply.

Her sucky day promised to improve, since she'd get to see Wade in an hour. Dodging Josh and the rest of his group all day at school took a lot of skill and effort. She'd had only one encounter with Lauren in the bathroom, and the girl seemed more freaked out than Iris.

She dropped her backpack on the floor. "Those smell delicious."

Gram shoveled a snickerdoodle cookie off her baking sheet with a metal spatula. Her auburn hair had lightened with all the gray hairs she'd gotten over the past year. "How was school, dear?"

Iris placed her keys on the counter by the door. "Torture. Like getting a tooth pulled without anesthetic. I don't know why they can't just leave me alone."

Gram paused, the snickerdoodle balancing on the spatula in her hand. "It's because there's something broken inside them. Until they face some tragedy of their own, they won't learn empathy. Best to steer clear of them, dear." She placed the cookie on the pile, reached over the counter, and patted Iris's hand before returning to her task. "I hate seeing any of my girls suffer. I wish there was something I could do to help. Know that you are loved here."

"I know." Iris shrugged a shoulder. "I probably deserve it anyway. I haven't always been the nicest person. Thanks for baking these." She snatched up a cookie, tore off a small piece, and popped the steaming goodness into her mouth. "They're Wade's favorite. Maybe I can at least get him to like me again. Too bad Aster can't change my fate back. It would be a lot easier. If I could just tell him that it wasn't my choice to break up with him, he would give us another chance."

"I'm so sorry, dear, but we must protect your sister. This isn't a secret we can share with others." Gram picked up a box of tinfoil, tore off a long sheet, and wrapped the plate of cookies. When she was done, she looked up at Iris, the corners of her mouth tugging into that warm smile that held so much concern and love for others. "Wade is a good boy. He'll see how you've changed and come to his senses."

Iris brushed the crumbs from her hands. "I hope you're right."

Something heavy slid across the floor upstairs.

"Is someone here?" Iris asked.

"Oh, I forgot," Gram said and glanced at the ceiling as if she could see whoever it was upstairs. "It's Violet. Your dad brought her home this afternoon. He put your boxes in Aster's room and her things in the garage apartment."

Excitement rushed through Iris. She'd been lonely with her twin gone. Violet had stayed with their father in Baltimore after classmates bullied her, sending photos of her and her girlfriend, Dena, making out without their shirts. It was spread all over school with an anonymous app. It had been screenshot and shared so many times, the school couldn't prove who originally posted the photograph.

But it wasn't the pic so much as the online bullying and jeers behind Violet's back at school that broke her. Dena was different than Violet. She couldn't care less what people said or thought about her.

"I leave tomorrow for North Carolina to help out your aunt with the move and Nathan," Gram was saying. "Poor dear, she has her hands full. The little tike is walking and climbing up things. Your dad will stay with you girls while your mom is away."

"Yeah, *stay*."

Nana raised an eyebrow at Iris's sarcastic tone.

"You mean at the Holiday Inn," Iris continued. "Why does that woman have to be so jealous? Why can't he stay in the guest room? He's our dad."

"Her name is Shelby, not *that woman*," Nana said. "Be nice. She's your stepmother. And I don't know why it matters to her when your mother is out of town."

"What does someone do at a florist convention, anyway?"

"I suppose learn new techniques and arrangements. It's good for your mother to take a break from the flower shop." Gram began spooning cookie dough onto the empty baking sheet.

Iris picked up her backpack. "I think I'll go up and see how Violet's doing and unpack some boxes before Wade comes over."

"Good idea," she said. "And remember, no telling your father or Wade about fate changing. Aster is done with it, and we must protect her. Besides, they wouldn't believe you if you did."

"Got it," Iris said. But she was pretty sure she could get Wade to believe it. He knew her. She wasn't some psychotic girl who believed in hocus pocus stuff. It might take her some time to convince him, but he'd come around if she stood her ground. She'd think of a way later. Right now, she had something else to deal with. Violet.

With each step up the back stairs, anxiety twitched inside Iris. She'd seen Violet several times on weekend visits to Baltimore and holidays at Gram's, but Violet barely spoke to her at first. As time passed and therapist bills multiplied, Violet and Iris had become close again. But would being home bring back memories of the incident? And would Violet blame Iris for being part of the group that bullied her?

Iris stood at the open door to the room she used to share with Violet. Her twin wrestled a shirt onto a hanger. The floorboard squeaked under Iris's foot as she adjusted, and Violet's gaze went to the door. They stared at each other for several seconds before Violet's face lit up in a smile and she rushed over. They hugged, and Iris wanted to cry with relief.

"I missed you tons," Violet said, releasing her.

Iris exhaled and glanced around the room at the empty boxes. "I'm so happy you're home. I was going to help you out, but it looks like you're done unpacking already."

"I am," she said. "Let me hang this up and I'll help you unpack yours."

"Sounds like a plan." Iris waited just inside the door, not knowing if she should go in or leave. It was strange that she didn't feel like she belonged in the room Violet and she had shared for years. It was as if she were an intruder. "I'll be in Aster's…um, my room."

The hall seemed tighter with all her problems crowding her as she walked to her new room. Anger was just under the surface of the façade she presented to the world. She was mad that none of her troubles was because of something she'd done. It was Aster's fault. Iris and Wade would be living their happily-ever-after if it weren't for Aster and that damn fate-changing thing. Seriously. Why did she have to continue to pay the price for her sister's mistakes?

When she opened the door, a strange moan sounded as the air escaped. Iris shuddered. The room looked different without Aster's things in it.

It was smaller than the one she had shared with her twin. A neat pile of sheets and blankets sat on the bed next to the comforter and pillows. The closet door was left open and someone had already hung up all of Iris's clothes. Boxes holding her books and knickknacks were neatly stacked near the window seat.

Her sisters were growing up and separating. Iris missed all the fun they'd had hiding in Grams' large house and playing on its private beach. Like Aster's posters and pictures that used to hang on the walls, those days were gone now.

"Where should we start?" Violet said from behind her.

Iris moved into the room. "I guess the boxes."

"Okay," Violet said and knelt beside them. She opened the top box and looked inside. "Books. I'll do these. How do you want them arranged on the shelf?"

Though Violet was being kind, there was an uneasiness passing between them. Unspoken words the other one wanted to say again, no matter how many times they were said before.

I'm sorry, Violet. Iris had told her so many times, it probably irritated Violet.

It wasn't your fault. She selfishly wanted to hear Violet say it again to ease her mind.

Instead, Iris answered her. "I prefer my books lined tallest to shortest. Shelves organized by genre."

"That's right," Violet said with a laugh, picking up the box and carrying it to the bookcase. "How could I forget?"

Iris just shrugged. For years, they'd fought over how to arrange the books in their room. Violet wanted all the colors together, but Iris refused, preferring the spines lined by height.

The flaps of the box scratched together as Iris opened the next one. It held her collection of papier-mâché statues. She removed the first one of an elephant she had made last year. The box teetered and Iris caught it before it fell, her foot kicking against the bottom paneling in the window seat. The panel fell forward and clattered against the wooden floor.

Violet shot her a look. "Are you okay?"

"Yeah," Iris answered, dropping to her knees and picking up the panel. "But I think I broke the window seat." Peering inside the space, she spotted something white hidden in the back. She reached in and dragged it out.

"What is it?" Violet came over to her side.

"It looks like an old hatbox." Iris untied the satin taupe ribbon securing the lacey box and removed it. A tarot deck sat on top of a bunch of papers and notebooks. She picked it up and inspected it. A red braid was tied around it.

"Is that Aster's hair?"

"I think so."

Violet scooted away. "Put it back."

Iris gave her a questioning look. "Are you afraid? These can't hurt us. We're not fate changers like Aster."

"I know, but still." Violet stood. "That bookcase is dusty. I'm going to grab a rag and some polish. Put those away. They give me the creeps."

When she'd left the room, Iris untied the braid and opened the box. A hissing sound filled the quiet of the room, and she twisted around, looking for the origin of the noise.

Stop freaking out. It's just the radiator.

Iris slipped the cards out of the package. The black vines on the back almost seemed like they were pulsating. She touched the top card, and something pulled at her fingertips. The blue veins just under her pale skin slowly turned black like a dark, ominous creature slithering up her arm. Ice cut through her blood vessels.

She gasped and dropped the cards, dashing to the mirror. The black invader rippled beneath her skin, traveling up the cords of her neck, across her left cheek, and over her forehead, disappearing under her hairline. Fear strangled her throat and she couldn't scream.

Shuddering, she wrapped her arms around herself. She was so cold, but the room was warm.

That's it. Relax. I am here for you, a woman's craggy voice said.

Iris spun around, but she was alone in the room. "Who are you? Where are you?"

I am you, the voice answered.

"What?" She stared back in the mirror. The black veins were gone. "Shit. I'm seeing and hearing things." Rubbing her temples, she crossed the room and curled up on the bare mattress. She shivered and tugged the comforter over her. She must be getting sick with something.

A headache throbbed, so she closed her eyes.

Yes. Sleep while I get to know you better. Your desires will be mine.

The girl's wooden stool rocked a little with each of her movements, the legs unsteady on the bumpy brick floor. Her clothes were colorful and a line of metal coins dangled from the hem of the scarf wrapped around her head. Beautiful dark curls fell around her pale shoulders. She shuffled the worn, dirt-smudged tarot cards.

The dream was scary real. It was as if Iris were someone else.

"You have reading before?" the girl said in a seductive tone that Iris could barely hear over the loud voices, clanking, and footsteps coming from somewhere outside the room.

"This shall be the first." The young man sitting across from the girl was dressed in expensive-looking eighteenth- or nineteenth-century clothes.

Eighteenth. Definitely that century. Of course she'd know that. It was her dream after all.

Iris felt like an intruder, standing off to the side watching the girl and the guy. The glances passing between them made Iris want to tell them to get a room. The one they were in was just a small alcove with a colorful curtain separating it from the rest of the bar, or tavern, or whatever they called it back then.

The world was familiar to Iris. Like she'd been there before. She even knew the extremely good-looking guy sitting across from the girl, though it was the girl's first encounter with him.

Armand Van Buren.

A royal. The second son of a count. She'd seen him riding his horse through the streets and being mischievous with his friends in the market. All the girls, and some older women, were giddy when he visited the village.

Armand leaned over the table, looking at her with such longing in his blue eyes that it pleased the girl. "You aren't like the other readers," he said, taking a lock of her curly dark hair in his hand and studying it. "You're lovely. What is your age?"

"Nearly sixteen," she said.

He smiled, letting the strand of hair slip from his hand. "Marrying age."

Her cheeks flushed.

An older woman, closely resembling the girl, pulled aside the curtain. In the woman's other hand she carried a tray with several mugs on it. "Why does it take you so long, Crina? Give him the reading and come help me. He'd better pay you well for keeping you so long." She released the curtain and it swung shut.

A wicked grin sharpened the corners of Armand's mouth. He removed some gold coins from his waistcoat pocket and placed them on the table. "It is said you change fates."

Crina shot up from her seat. "Who told you these lies?"

He grabbed her hand. "Sit. You needn't worry. No one would believe the old woman."

She yanked her hand from his grasp. "Woman?"

"The one who sells dried lavender in the market." His light hair framed his face like the sun. Iris thought he totally resembled Leonardo DiCaprio in *Romeo and Juliet*.

"Bunică…"

Her grandmother? Iris wasn't sure how she knew that was who the girl meant.

"You know of her?" he said.

"I do." Crina sat back down, picked up the tarot deck, and fanned the cards across the table. "Choose one."

With his gaze on her, not bothering to look at the cards, he let his finger land on one. He slowly slid it out from the other cards and left it in the middle of the table. His smoldering eyes on Crina made Iris feel uneasy.

Crina flipped over the card. The picture was of a man with a crown and a long white beard sitting on a throne. "The Emperor reversed."

"What does it mean?"

"The image is facing away from you," Crina said. "Meaning you have lack of control. I see you as the second. Not the heir."

"That is true. My brother shall be count." His hand covered Crina's and she started. "Can you change that?"

Crina swallowed hard. "I cannot be certain what will happen to your brother if I do."

That sharp, devious grin crept across his face again. "I shall be solely at fault for whatever does."

The noises in the tavern seemed to fade. "Two more coins," she said.

He placed them on the table.

She picked up a red crystal and touched the Emperor with it. The card flew up in the air, hovering between Armand and Crina. The image on the card separated into two, and they spun in different directions until they slammed back together and the card dropped to the table.

"It is done…" Crina's voice faded and Iris fell into darkness.

A cold hand shook her arm. "Iris? Are you okay?" She opened her eyes. Violet stared down at her with concern pinching her face. "Why are Aster's cards spread across the floor?"

Iris sat up, her head feeling as heavy as a bowling ball. "I…I'm not sure." She scooted off the bed and picked up one of the cards. The vines against the purple background were now green. "I don't understand. They changed color."

"What are you talking about?"

Iris held up the card for Violet to see. "The vines. They were black before, right?"

"They're definitely green. Must have been a shadow on them before," Violet said, setting the polish and rag on top of the bookcase. "Oh, I forgot. Wade's here for you."

"Oh no." She combed her fingers through her ratty hair. "I have to fix this. Can you buy me some time? Tell him I'll be right down."

Violet headed for the door. "Will do."

Iris hurried around picking up the scattered cards. "And keep him company until I'm ready?"

"Sure thing." Violet hurried out the door.

Alone in the room, she had a sinking feeling as she gathered the last of the cards.

It's this room. Aster's room. That's it. I'm freaking out because of that damn fate-changing thing. But the dream felt real. The voice. The black thing under my skin.

"I seriously need some sleep," she said, tossing the tarot deck along with the braid of hair into the hatbox and putting it back in its hiding place under the window seat. Before going downstairs, she fixed her hair and cleaned away the mascara smudges under her eyes.

Iris took a deep breath. Why was she so nervous? This was Wade. Skinny Wade with the wide smile and warm eyes who she'd met in middle school. They knew everything about each other. Shared sandwiches when the other one would forget a lunch. He defended her freshman year when a group of sophomore guys teased her. Wade. The one who set off a million dragonflies in her stomach at his kiss. Wade. Her best friend.

And missing him was a sharp breath that cut through her chest.

But he wasn't skinny Wade anymore. He was smart. Had insanely perfect dark, wavy hair that he wore long, just below his chin. And she liked his hands. They were strong and showed signs of the work he did either on his bike or on the boat. Manly hands. Unlike Josh's, which were soft and somewhat feminine.

When she walked into the kitchen carrying her backpack, Violet and Wade were laughing.

She is flirting with him. The craggy voice was back. *She wants him.*

"No she doesn't," Iris said.

Violet and Wade turned their heads at hearing her.

"What did you say?" Violet asked.

Iris felt sick. *What the hell is happening to me?* "Nothing," she said, crossing the kitchen. "Thanks for keeping him company, Violet. Sorry I'm late."

"No worries," he said, leaning back in his chair. "It's your dime."

Your dime? He is only here because you pay him. The voice scraped across Iris's ears, sending a shudder down her spine.

Iris tightened her grasp around the strap of her backpack. *Shut up and get out of my head!*

As you wish. But I could help you with that boy.

"I don't need your help," Iris responded.

Wade stood and grabbed his jacket off the back of the chair. "Hey, I'm here only because you're paying me. If you don't need my help, fine. I have better things to do."

"No, no, I didn't mean you." Iris placed her hand on his arm to stop him. Touching him sent a flurry of nerves through her stomach. "I do need your help."

"You meant me?" Violet sprang to her feet. "You're acting so strange today. I was just keeping Wade company." She stomped off and up the back stairs.

"Well, that's a good start to a first day back." Wade draped his jacket over the chair before sitting back down.

"Yeah," Iris said, pulling out a seat beside him and plopping down. "This day blows so far."

I've seriously lost it.

Wade picked up a cookie from the plate in the middle of the table. "So what do you want to tackle first?"

His eyes were like probes into her soul. Adjusting uneasily in her chair, she removed her math book, notebook, and pencil from her bag. How was she going to survive this? Having him act as if they were only acquaintances was worse than not seeing him at all.

"Thanks for agreeing to do math, too," she said, flipping the page to her assignment and semiconsciously aware of putting the end of her pencil between her teeth.

"You made an offer I couldn't refuse," he said with a wink. "What are we working on?"

"This," she said, sliding the open book across the table so he could see.

He leaned closer to view the page. She could smell the snickerdoodles on his breath and the light cologne he always wore. His knee rubbing against hers caused her to hold her breath. She was afraid to move, to break the connection, to feel the coldness rush back to her.

"Precalculus," he said. "Nice."

"There's nothing nice about it in my opinion." Iris released her breath and slumped back in her chair.

He bumped her shoulder. "Come on. Cheer up. Once you catch on, it'll be easy."

It was doubtful she'd catch on, but with him around, she'd at least have fun failing.

Chapter Four

WADE

Watching Iris with the eraser of her pencil between her teeth as she tried to figure out the equation on the page drove Wade insane. The gloss on her bottom lip glistened against the light coming from the overhead lamp in the kitchen. It seemed like she was having a hard time concentrating.

Wade cleared his throat. "Do you need more help?"

"It makes no sense." Iris sighed. "Why do we need this stuff?"

Wade laughed and grabbed a cookie, which was probably his sixth one. Whenever he was nervous, he'd take one to keep her from noticing. "It comes in handy for many jobs."

She gave him her frustrated look, which only succeed at tugging Wade's insides. "Not any I plan on doing."

"Let's see what you have so far," he said, reaching for her paper, their hands brushing against each other causing Iris to jump a little, and he chuckled under his breath. She was uneasy around him. He liked that. At least he wasn't the only one.

She pulled the paper out of his reach. "No. You'll think I'm dumb."

Her flushed cheeks and the way she leaned in his direction was a sure sign she was into him. All she had to do now was twirl her hair around her finger and he'd be positive. He'd seen her do it many times when she liked a guy.

Iris twirled a long strand of strawberry-blond hair around her finger.

Wade smiled, flattered that she was trying her moves on him. "I won't think that," he said. "Why are you paying me? I'm your tutor. You have to show me your work. I don't care if you're dumb."

She stopped twirling her hair and straightened—an angry look on her face.

"Oh no," he quickly said. "I didn't mean that. I meant… Wait. You're the one who said you were dumb. I just repeated you."

"Right." She returned her focus to her book.

Great. Now who's the dumb one? Wade picked up another cookie, trying to act like that didn't just happen. But she obviously wasn't going to forget it. She was leaning away from him, a scowl still on her face. Before their breakup, she'd call him on his stupidity. They'd joke about it.

Her hot-and-cold reaction to him was confusing, as if he'd been on a roller coaster with her. First, she dumped Josh and declared her love for Wade, and, a few days later, she was back with Josh. Then suddenly it was off with Josh again. No explanations. No apologies for smashing whatever they'd had. How could he ever trust her again?

It was hot while it lasted. He really thought Iris was his soul mate. And here he was, taking her shit again.

"Listen," he finally said. "If you want to reconsider this deal, it's cool. I don't need the money that badly."

Iris leaned back in her chair. "I'm sorry. I don't feel like myself today. It's been stressful lately. And…and…" She looked up at him with those big eyes the color of the summer sky over the Ocean City boardwalk. They captivated him. So much so, it was hard to stay mad at her. "Josh and his friends," she said. "They're such bullies. I can take it, but I'm worried about Violet."

He placed his hand on hers, and her fingers jerked a little. He liked what his touch did to her. "You don't have to worry about Violet. Dena has her back."

She flipped her hair over her shoulder and twisted to look at him directly. The movement was so hot it caused Wade to gulp. There was something in her stare. Was it longing? When she leaned closer, he was certain she wanted him. He wouldn't be able to stop himself if he stayed there any longer.

He pushed his chair away from the table and stood. "I need the bathroom. Work on the problem while I'm gone."

She gave him that disappointed look again, then picked up her pencil and studied the paper in front of her. He looked back when he reached the entryway and caught her watching his retreat. She quickly returned her attention to her work.

What game is she playing? Her moods were confusing him. One minute she was scowling, the next she was checking him out.

Her actions the last few months made him believe he could have her back if he wanted. And there was no denying that he did want her. Who wouldn't? There was much more to her than a pretty face and banging body. She was talented and kind and cared for causes like the environment and smart, no matter what she thought. He could give it another go with her, but he'd be crazy if he did. There was no ignoring the trust issue. He would always worry she'd have a change of heart again. Run off with some other guy, or worse, go back to Josh.

In the bathroom behind the front staircase, he washed

his face. What he needed to do was cool down. Every inch of Iris played across his mind. Her upturned nose with a dusting of freckles. Her slender fingers grasping a paintbrush as she created the most beautiful paintings. Her laughter that sounded like some sort of high-pitched song. The sexy way she swayed when she walked. All these thoughts drove him insane.

From a dispenser on the sink, he tugged out a disposable towel, dried his face, and tossed the used paper in the trash. As he came out of the bathroom, Violet stepped off the stairs.

"Hey, do you have a second?" she whispered.

Wade nodded, following her to a room on the other side of the staircase. "What's up?"

She closed the door behind him. "I'm not supposed to tell you this." She paced, then stopped and looked up at him. "It wasn't Iris's fault...the whole breakup thing. She had no control."

"What do you mean? Did your parents make her break up with me?"

"Keep your voice down," she said, adjusting on her feet and wringing her hands. "It's not like that. I can't tell you. But I know she's heartbroken and misses you. When she would come and visit me in Baltimore, she'd cry at night over losing you. Won't you give her another chance?"

"Why can't you tell me the reason she ended things?" he pressed. "And why did she get back with Josh right after our breakup? She didn't even wait an hour."

"I can't tell you," she said, louder than a whisper now. "I know it sounds sketchy, but if you don't trust her, will you trust me?"

Wade rubbed the back of his neck. "You want me to trust you, but you won't say why she had no control over breaking up with me? This is bullshit." He turned and opened the door. "I have to go."

He rushed to the kitchen and picked up his jacket. "So, I'm going to head out."

Iris glanced at him, a startled look on her face. "You didn't check this last equation."

"Okay, let me see." He leaned over and slid the paper across the table to see it better, catching a hint of Iris's shampoo on her hair. Floral. Like everything else in her home. And it drove him insane. "You got it. Nice job."

"I did?" The excitement in her voice softened his frustration.

"Yep."

"Thank you so much," she said. "Should I pay you now or do you want to get paid weekly?"

"Weekly is fine." The less words he spoke, the better for him. He had to get out of there and release some steam. But those eyes. Those fucking eyes with so much beauty and kindness paused him. They were so familiar to him yet still mysterious.

"Iris…"

"Yes?"

He took her hands and pulled her up to her feet. Cradling her head in his grasp, he stared at her, wanting desperately to kiss her, to feel the softness of her lips again. Her hands traveled up his chest to his shoulders.

What am I doing?

He wanted her more than breathing. Wanted to go back to the days before her betrayal. But she'd hurt him. He pushed away from her.

"What's wrong?" she said breathlessly, reaching for him.

He backed away. "I can't do this." He shook his head and stormed out the kitchen door, tugging on his jacket as he headed for his motorcycle. He lifted the seat, grabbed his helmet, and shoved it on his head, vaguely aware of Iris calling out to him. With one swift move, he straddled the seat and slipped on his leather gloves. At the press of the start button, the bike growled to life. He released the clutch and took off down the street.

Thoughts of Iris pelted his brain. Iris smiling, her front teeth overlapping just slightly. Iris laughing, a cute snort slipping out at times.

Iris.

What does she expect from me? How can I trust her?

He rode in and out of the blooms of light coming from the streetlamps, going from light to dark. Just like his emotions. Get back with Iris. Don't.

Stop thinking about her.

Iris sharing her lunch with him when he'd forgotten his in eighth grade. Iris smudging paint on his face while he watched her at her easel, when he liked her as more than friends and she liked someone else. Iris telling him she loved him and no one else. Iris ignoring his phone calls. Iris texting him that she and Josh had made up, not even bothering to explain things to him.

Iris.

Fucking Iris.

Fuck.

He pulled a U-turn, speeding the bike back in the direction he had come.

Iris bringing him homemade soup from her gram when he was sick. Iris decorating his home with his mother for every single one of his birthdays since they'd become friends. Iris sending him heart grams for Valentine's Day. Iris wearing a Santa hat to deliver him presents at Christmas.

Iris.

Wade stopped in front of her house, turned off his bike, and set the kickstand. He bounded up the steps without pause, rang the doorbell, and waited.

And waited.

He removed his helmet. It sure was taking a long time for someone to answer. Just as he turned to leave, thinking that he was probably a sucker to believe they could get back what they had, the door finally opened.

"Wade," Iris said with a shaky voice.

The mascara smudged under her eyes told him she'd been crying. It was a sign she cared and that maybe they could work on it. And he hated hurting her.

"Okay," he said.

"What?" She looked confused.

"Friends. We can try it. See where it takes us." He pulled his hand through his hair. "I'll continue to tutor you. No cost."

"Really? That would be great." Her voice was full of hope. "But I am paying you for the tutoring."

"No. I can't take your money, Iris. We've been friends for years." Gazing down at that face of hers melted him. Even with teary eyes, mascara smudges, and red nose, she was beautiful. Lost in a world that consisted of only them, he almost forgot his fears...his anger. Almost. When they were together, he was certain he could forgive her, but once they were apart, the doubt would always come rushing back. "And we can't kiss," he said. "It gets confusing."

Her eyebrows crinkled together. "I didn't do anything. You were about to kiss me."

He tapped his helmet against his leg. "Well, you gave me those looks."

"What looks?" She acted innocent.

"You know the ones."

"Seriously? I can't help it." Even the expression she gave him when she thought he was acting crazy was a turn-on.

He dropped his helmet and quickly snatched it up. "Just act like you would around Carys. Okay?"

"Sure."

"So, friends?" he said.

"Friends," she repeated.

They stood there in an awkward silence for several beats until he couldn't take it any longer. "Okay." He turned from her and said over his shoulder as he was leaving, "I'll see you at school tomorrow."

"Okay. See you then." Her voice was quiet and uncertain sounding.

He gave her a slight wave with his gloved hand before speeding off again. *Maybe this time she won't shred my heart.*

Chapter Five

Iris

Even with the cool autumn breeze, Iris was hot. Almost as though she had a fever. She flung the covers off her body. Her thoughts of Wade and his almost-kiss kept playing in her head. She was excited that he agreed to be friends, but at the same time, she was disappointed he wanted to be *just* friends. She worried they'd never get back what they had before. With a yawn, she stretched her arms over her head.

That's right. Wake up. The craggy voice was back.

Iris sat up and searched the dark room. "Who are you? And where are you?"

I am a friend. Josh and his lackeys—you want revenge. I am here to help you.

"You're in my mind, aren't you?" Iris grabbed her head and squeezed. "Oh my God, I'm going insane."

We're not going to hurt them…too badly. Now, get Aster's tarot cards.

"No. Get out of my head!" She fell back on the mattress

and covered her head with her pillow as if she could hide from the tormenting voice.

Don't fight me, Iris. You will lose. I will not ask again.

A sharp pain stabbed Iris's skull, and she held her head tighter. The pain increased until she was sure that every single vein in her brain would burst. "*Ahhh*...no, no, *no*. Please stop. I'll get them. *Please*." The pain subsided, and Iris slowly stood. Her stomach was queasy and her legs unsteady.

Iris crossed the throw rug to the window seat and removed the panel. It clanked against the wooden floor as she set it down. She dragged the hatbox out from its hiding place, undid the ribbon, and took out the deck, putting the box back in the cubby space and resetting the panel. Climbing back in bed, she sat cross-legged on the sheets.

"Now what?" she asked her empty room.

Lauren. Now an enemy, once a friend. What shall be her end?

"End?" Panic fluttered in her chest. "What do you mean? I don't want her to die. And she's still a friend. I don't want to hurt her."

Silly girl. I only used "end" to rhyme with "friend." The punishment shall fit the crime. Flip the cards. Let's see what we have to work with, shall we?

"You have the wrong sister." Iris dropped the box on the bed. "I'm not a fate changer."

Not to worry. The voice was firm and scary. *I am. Do as I say or you will suffer greatly.*

Iris removed the cards from the box and turned them over one at a time. The images were familiar yet foreign to her. She'd seen them when Miri had tested her to see if she was a fate changer. Illustrations of kings, queens, knights, and paupers adorned the cards. Some had yellow circles with stars in the middle on them—Miri had called them pentacles—some had swords, other wands, and the rest cups. She had called them suits like with playing cards. Iris flipped over another one.

Stop. The Hermit card. Isolation. Upside down—the reverse fate—withdrawn, edgy, cold… Yes. This is perfect. She abandoned you, so we shall isolate her.

Iris picked up the card. An old man in a cloak that matched his gray beard with the hood over his head held a walking stick in one hand and a lantern in the other. The tips of Iris's fingers burned where she held the card. She turned it. The vines on the back went from green to black.

Say her name.

"No. What's happening?"

Say her name.

"No."

SAY HER NAME! The voice, so loud and angry, stabbed at her brain.

Tears burned Iris's eyes, flooding them and making the image on the card blurry.

"Lauren." It was a whisper, a soft squeak of a sound. Iris wasn't even sure she was the one who spoke it.

Now, tomorrow, hand her the card. That is all you must do. The curse will take care of the rest.

"Who are you?"

Who am I?

Was this how insanity was for those inflicted with it? Unable to get the voices out of their heads? Would she have to live with this crazy old woman's voice forever?

I used to know who I was. A long time ago. A heartbreak. A young woman scorned. An eye for an eye. Some say revenge is sweet. I say it is like a heavy cream and sugar dessert. Delicious and satisfying.

"You're evil."

Now that entirely depends on what side of evil you reside.

Iris's entire body quaked, and she gasped for air. The

room seemed like it was closing in on her. Where was the voice coming from? She covered her ears and shouted, "Stop it. Leave me alone."

She lay on the bed watching the ceiling for so many minutes she lost count. The voice was gone. Her heartbeats were so strong and painful against her chest, the sound of it thumping loudly in her ears. She grabbed the pillow from behind her and hugged it tight, trying to stop her arms and legs from shaking. Her mom was gone, and Gram would be leaving early in the morning. They didn't need to know she was completely losing it. She had to be sick and it was making her hear things. That's why she was shivering. Why she was cold all the time. Of course, that was it. Definitely the flu.

She rolled onto her other side, watching the shadows of leaves on the tree outside flutter on her wall until finally falling asleep, the darkness wrapping her in a cool autumn-night embrace.

Crina pushed down her skirts, watching Armand tie his trousers together. Cold mud caked her backside. Her mother would be angry.

The meadow glistened with the aftermath of the morning rain. The river angrily jumped over the rocks. A small patch of thick grass under the canopy of a large copper beech tree had become their love nest.

"I will not be able to meet you for some time," Armand said, picking up his waistcoat from the ground. "An uncle and his family are coming from the north. There will be several days of celebrations."

A pout formed on Crina's lips as she wrapped her shawl around her shoulders. "You could sneak away."

"I will try." He gently kissed her lips. "Being apart from

you will be maddening. My brother is to marry our cousin. She is such an annoyance, but it is his duty, being the heir."

"And you?" She kissed him again. "Can you marry as you please?"

"No, but I have no duty here." He smiled down at her. "As soon as I have enough money gathered, we shall leave this place. I will marry you. Make our fortune in America."

"I will go wherever you wish," she said. "Promise me again. You will marry me."

He pulled her close to him, pressed his lips to hers, and released her. "I promise."

Lockers slammed, voices commanded, and the noises grated down Iris's spine. The voice and dreams she'd been having lately had her in a trance. She wasn't herself. There was something inside her, crowding her mind and pressing against her chest until she could hardly breathe.

The tarot card felt like a lead weight in her hoodie's pocket. It was stupid for her to think that giving the card to Lauren would cause something bad to happen to her. But Iris knew what tarot cards and the magic behind them could do. She had experienced it firsthand. Her own fate had been changed and her life destroyed. How could she do that to someone else?

She put her math book inside her locker and slammed the door. And there was Wade, heading down the hall, combing his fingers through his helmet hair. She couldn't face him. Couldn't let him see the darkness clouding her. With her eyes on him, making sure he hadn't spotted her, she ducked into the girls' bathroom.

Girls crowded around the mirror as they fixed makeup they'd applied only an hour ago before leaving their homes.

Iris stood by the door, pretending to check her text messages on her iPhone. Group by group went out the door until Iris was alone. She placed her books on top of the towel dispenser and checked her reflection in what passed for a mirror above the sink.

A dark smudge or something was on her forehead. She rubbed at the mark, but it wouldn't go away. She leaned closer to the mirror. It was a vein—a *black* one. Her heart raced and she lost her breath. The vein moved when she ran her finger across it, and she jumped back, gasping for air.

Find Lauren and give her the tarot card.

"No. I'm not playing this game." Iris grabbed her books, tugged open the door, and darted into the hall.

You cannot get rid of me. I am inside you.

Iris concentrated. *Leave me alone.*

The voice cackled and the sound vibrated through Iris's head, hurting her ears and making her clench her teeth. When the voice was around, Iris could hear a nasally breathing like white noise over her thoughts.

If you refuse to help me, I will go it alone.

It suddenly went silent in her head. The loud breathing no longer there. Iris heaved a deep sigh.

She brushed off the crazy woman's voice as fear. Violet had creeped her out so hard about Aster's tarot cards being evil that Iris was now hearing things. It reminded her of when she was younger and they would watch scary movies. It would take Iris days to get over being scared. She decided that she'd tie that braided hair rope around those cards and hide the box in the garage apartment. Aster could deal with them when she came home for winter break.

The first bell rang and she rushed to her class. Wade stood outside the door, a backpack on his shoulder. A smile spread across his face when he spotted her approaching.

"Hey," he said when she reached him.

"Hi." She tucked her hand in her pocket. The card. It was still there. She quickly tugged her hand out, losing all focus on Wade. Lauren was in her first class, and Iris worried about what the voice had asked her to do. She looked past Wade and down the hall that led to Lauren's locker. There was no sign of her yet.

"You okay?" Wade asked.

Iris pulled her stare away and glanced up at him. His eyebrows pinched together as he studied her.

"Yeah, I'm fine," she said. "Just a little distracted. I didn't sleep well last night."

Wade frowned. "Yeah, me, too."

He thinks it's because of him, Iris thought.

Iris wanted to feel that giddy thing inside her that seeing him usually caused, but the voice and the tarot card waiting in her pocket prevented it.

When she hadn't said anything, he continued. "You want to join Dena and me for lunch?"

She made her best effort at a genuine smile. "I'd love to."

He glanced around.

She lowered her head and stared at the speckled floor tiles.

Neither one knew what to say.

"Cool," he finally said when the silence between them was getting uncomfortable. "Don't grab anything at the food counter. I packed us something."

She looked up, startled. "You did?"

"Listen, I'm not sure what happened to make you break up with me. Violet said—"

"What did she say?" Iris asked. Did her sister tell him about fate changing?

A concerned look crossed his face. "She just said it was something out of your control. I don't get why you went back to Josh. You should have come to me. Was it what we heard my mom say? Why you ended things?"

He thinks it's because of that? A few days before their breakup, Iris and Wade had been making out in his living room with the lights off when his mom came home. She was on her cell phone telling someone on her campaign that Wade would date whoever he wanted. She had said that Iris was a good girl. It was awkward, but Iris would never end things with him because of it.

"Was it because you thought that person on the phone with my mom could hurt her campaign?" He stared down at her.

Maybe if she didn't say anything, he'd go on believing that was the reason and she wouldn't have to lie to him.

"Anyway, it doesn't matter anymore." He looked down the hall. "I should go. Don't want to get another tardy slip. See you at lunch," he said before jogging off.

She turned to watch his retreat. He was wearing her favorite jeans. The ones that made his butt look good. His worn leather jacket finished off that perfect rebel look. Dena liked to tease him about looking like one of the *Bandidos* in that jacket, which Iris had to Google. It was a Mexican biker gang, and it would make Wade angry when Dena would say that, since he was Cuban.

The way Wade dressed didn't match the person he was. He was a good guy, beyond smart, and he always stood up for others. Not to mention, he was a phenomenal cook. Her stomach grumbled at the thought of lunch later.

Lauren, lugging an overstuffed backpack on her shoulder and glancing at her iPhone, ran past Wade. As she approached and noticed Iris standing there, the smile she'd had while looking at her screen slipped. She slowed her steps, spotting something on the floor.

"Is this yours," she said, reaching for the Hermit tarot card.

"Wait." Iris tried to snatch it up before Lauren, but she was a second too late.

Lauren quickly dropped the card. "Ow, it shocked me."

No! It must've fallen out when I put my hand in my pocket.

The bell rang, startling Lauren. She brushed by Iris and went into the classroom, leaving the card on the floor.

Iris picked it up, the entire world sinking around her. The vines on the backside of the card were green again. *Oh please, don't hurt her.* She pleaded with the voice, but there was no answer.

"Are you coming inside, Miss Layne?" Mrs. Chapman asked from where she stood at the front of the class. Iris made her way to her desk, her eyes on Lauren, who was rubbing the fingers that had touched the card.

What did you do? Iris asked the invader in her head, again.

Still, there was no answer. No craggy voice. No annoying breathing. No thoughts. Just that sinking feeling that made Iris hold her stomach as she slipped into the seat at her desk.

Chapter Six

WADE

For the fifth time, Dena sucked the air out of her empty water bottle and then released it, the plastic popping back into its original form. The crinkling noise grated on Wade's nerves and it was bugging the shit out of him. He grabbed the bottle from her.

She reached for it. "Hey, what's up with you?"

"It's annoying." Wade tossed it at a nearby trash can. It hit the rim and landed on the ground.

"Nice," Dena said. "Good thing you quit basketball."

"Funny." Wade shuffled over and picked up the bottle. He had left the team because of Josh. Not that he was afraid of Josh, but because he didn't want to kill the loser. He dropped the bottle in the can and turned to head back. Iris and Violet were walking their way.

Though they were identical, Iris's hair was darker and longer, and she was curvier than Violet. Iris was slightly shorter, too. They both had a habit of wrinkling their noses when they were nervous and had the cutest freckles like the rest of the Layne girls.

Dena shot to her feet and trotted over to them, wrapping her arms around Violet and stretching up to plant a kiss on her lips. Iris kept walking until she met Wade. He wasn't sure what to do. Shake her hand? Hug? No. He opted for handing her the can of Dr Pepper he'd gotten her.

"Where's Carys?" he asked.

"She has a senate meeting." Iris took the can. "Thanks."

They were quiet for many seconds, not knowing what to say to each other—again.

"Well, I hope you're in the mood for my famous *mixto* sandwiches," he said.

She squinted against the sun. "Are you kidding? I don't know what I missed more—you or them."

Her words smacked him like a surge of wind hitting a sail, leaving him breathless. *She missed me.* He wanted to admit he felt the same way, but that damn fear that she'd hurt him again prevented it.

"I think I'm *flattered*?" he said instead and slid onto the bench of the stone picnic table, patting the seat beside him.

She hesitated, looking back at Violet and Dena, who were still lip-locked. The six months away from school and her therapist sessions had really given Violet the confidence to be herself. But Iris knew her sister. By the way Violet's eyes shifted around, not completely focused on Dena, she was still nervous about PDAs.

"Okay, you two," Wade called to them. "Our lunch break isn't that long."

They separated and held hands as they strolled over to the picnic table. "What's for lunch?" Dena said, stepping over the bench and plopping down. Violet sat and nestled up to Dena's side.

Wade slid two tinfoil-wrapped sandwiches over to them.

"Remember, you owe me a pizza for this."

"Hey, I'm not the one who wanted to impress Iris with my *mixto*-making skills," Dena said.

Wade kicked her under the table.

"Ouch!" Dena glared at him.

"I wasn't trying to *impress* anyone," Wade said. "I just like to cook."

"I know," Iris said. "Thank you for making them."

"You're welcome," he said, holding Dena's stare.

Dena picked up the bundles and handed one to Violet, then unwrapped the other one. "*Mixto* sandwiches. My day is made."

Violet inspected hers. "What's a *mixto* sandwich?"

Dena passed her a water bottle. "It's a pressed sandwich made out of Cuban bread, stuffed with ham, roasted pork, pickles, and Swiss cheese."

"Some call it a Cubano," Wade added.

"And these," she said, picking up a chip from a plastic container Wade had just opened and placed in the middle of the table, "are plantain chips." She took a bite of her sandwich.

Iris smiled at Wade. "It all looks delicious."

He could get lost in her smile. It lit up her face and sparkled in her eyes. Hanging out as friends was going to be hard when all he wanted to do was take her in his arms and show her how much he wanted her.

She undid the foil from her sandwich and took a big bite. There was nothing hotter than a girl chowing down on a *mixto*. A little mustard stained the corner of her mouth and she wiped it away with her fingertips.

"This is so fricking good," she said with a full mouth, covering her lips with her hand.

"Glad you like it," he said, handing her a napkin. "It's better when they're hot."

"Dude, you outdid yourself," Dena said. "Cold or hot,

doesn't matter."

Wade snatched up his can of cola and took a long sip. "You two seem all right. How'd you do it? You know, after the shit that went down?"

Violet lowered her sandwich. "Counseling. Finally accepting who I am. So it's a pic of me in my bra. Who cares? It's like a bathing suit. I was kissing someone I really love. And the bullies online, they're just haters." She put her hand on Dena's hand. "It was dumb to let them get to me."

It hurt enough for her to try to kill herself. They all knew Josh's gang had shared that photograph online. They'd made a humiliating graphic with it, slut-shaming her. No anonymous app could hide that fact. But they couldn't prove it. If Wade wouldn't be suspended and hurt his mother's campaign for a senate position, he'd beat the shit out of Josh and a few of his douchebag friends. Dena had tried. Didn't do too well. Ended up with a black eye and busted lip. She had succeeded in getting Josh suspended for a few days with her, which forced the coach to bench him at the following hometown basketball game.

Iris picked at a slice of ham sticking out of her sandwich, a frown on her face.

Wade knew what Iris was thinking. She was part of the group that had hurt her sister. Though she hadn't had anything to do with it and she immediately went to the principal's office to rat them out, she still felt responsible. It didn't help that the jerks only got a slap on the hand because there was no proof they'd done it.

"So any big plans for the weekend?" Wade asked, hoping a change of subject would brighten the mood.

Dena took up Violet's hand and cradled it in her own. "My girl and I are doing dinner and a movie. We've been apart for far too long. We need to celebrate her return to school. Right?"

"Yes. It's so great to be back." A wide smile spread across Violet's lips—one that said, *I'm trying so hard to please everyone right now*. She was faking it. He could tell by the way her eyes, clouded with fear, darted around the courtyard, most likely looking for her tormentors.

Iris gave Violet a curious look. They had their own language. Could feel what the other felt. Even with the wedge of distrust splitting them apart, their connection was still there.

Each of their cell phones suddenly went off—Dena's rap song blared, Iris's chimed, and Violet's and his vibrated against the table. A look passed among them before they each picked up their phones and checked the notice.

"Holy shit," Dena said, scrolling down her screen. "Who is that?"

"Lauren," Iris said, barely above a whisper.

It was a collage of pictures of Lauren at a party posted on her InstaPik by Marsha Simmons. There was one with Lauren making out with Josh. Several of her drinking and snuggling up to him. Written in all caps in the caption below the main pic were: WHORE. DON'T TRUST HER. WORST FRIEND EVER. The comments from others kept popping up. Wade scrolled down them, and every single one was mean and hateful toward Lauren.

Violet scrambled over the bench seat. "This has got to stop," she said and stormed off.

Iris grabbed her backpack and ran after her.

It took Dena several seconds to register what was happening before she jumped up, grabbed her and Violet's packs, and went after them.

Wade heaved a sigh, gathered the remains of their lunch, and tossed it in the trash can before following the others. When he reached them, Violet had her arms around a crying Lauren, yelling at a group jeering at her.

"Stop it." Violet's glare darted over the many faces in the

crowd. "You're all cruel. How would you feel if someone did this to you? Josh and his gang do this to everyone. Most of you have been victims of their hate before. You should all be ashamed of yourselves."

Iris was against the lockers with tears in her eyes.

Lauren's head rested on Violet's shoulder. "I don't remember anything," she said, sniffling.

Anger hit Wade like a punch to the gut. The boys in his Big Brother club acted more mature than the privileged dumbasses at their school. He fisted his hands and marched over to Violet's side.

"Get out of here," he yelled, his eyes scanning the crowd. Most rushed off, except for Josh, Marsha, and some guys from the basketball team. He fixed his eyes on Josh. Dena stepped in front of him, her hands on his chest stopping him from going at him. "You think it's funny," he said over Dena's shoulder. "Hurting people like this. You best watch your back. 'Cause you'll get yours someday. Karma's a bitch."

"What are you doing with Iris?" Perry leaned against the locker beside Josh and Marsha. His lanky body towered over them. He rubbed the black stubble on his head, flicking his gaze over at Josh like a puppy looking for praise from his master. "You like Josh's leftovers or what?" He cracked up at his own lame joke.

Wade was ready to smack Perry. He pushed against Dena, and she pushed back. "You don't want to go there. You'll be suspended. Remember the campaign."

"Who are you, my mom?" Wade hissed.

"You wish," Dena said. "Come on, man, use your common sense."

Wade backed up. "Okay, okay. I'm done."

Josh flung his arm around Marsha's shoulders. "Let's get out of here."

Marsha had a smug smile on her face. "That'll teach you

to mess with someone else's boyfriend."

"You're an idiot," Wade said to her. "It doesn't look like he's fighting her off in those pictures. You might want to put a leash on him. He's a dog, after all."

"Whatever," Marsha said, Josh pulling her along with him.

Perry followed, flashing his goofy smile over his shoulder at them.

"Come on." Violet let Lauren go, slipped her hand into hers, and led her down the hall.

Lauren glanced around, mascara running like black rivers from her teary eyes. "Where are we going?"

"To the office."

Wade shuffled over to Iris. "You okay?"

"It's my fault." She slid down the locker and sat on her heels, her bottom eyelids holding a pool of tears. She blinked and they ran down her cheeks.

He squatted in front of her, taking her trembling hands in his own. "None of this is your fault. You're no longer part of that group."

She sniffled. "You don't understand."

"Then help me to. Why are you torturing yourself like this?"

"I don't even…" She stood and Wade went up with her. "I want to tell you, but I can't."

"Wish you would," he said.

She smiled, but it wasn't genuine, it was pained. "I'll be okay. It's nothing really. I'm just a little insane lately."

"Well, I could have told you that." He chuckled.

A small laugh escaped her lips. "Guess you could."

She was anything but okay. Was she losing it? He had an urge to hug her but stopped himself. They'd come to a place where he was afraid to touch her. Afraid to let his feelings be known.

Those big eyes of hers looked up at him, and he wanted to take her away from there. Take her somewhere where he could show her exactly how he felt about her.

The end of lunch bell rang, and Iris pulled her hands away from his. Even when crying, she had this natural beauty to her. One of innocence and something a poet could describe better than he could.

"So, you want to come out to the boat?" He plunged his hand into his backpack and retrieved a napkin. "Friday night?"

She sniffled. "Are you asking me on a date?"

"Yeah, sort of a date, I guess." He handed her the napkin.

"I'd like that." She wiped her eyes with it, then hoisted her bag onto her shoulder. "Thanks for lunch. See you later, then?"

"Yep."

Wade rubbed the back of his neck as he watched Iris until she disappeared around the corner leading to the next hall over. Something was off with her. She seemed distracted. Lost.

Not wanting another tardy slip, he jogged off for his next class across campus, worrying about Iris, worrying about taking another chance with her, worrying about pretty much fucking everything.

Chapter Seven

Iris

Iris slammed her bedroom door, locked it, and dropped her backpack on the floor. "Where are you? You get inside my head when I don't want you there and jump ship when I want to talk to you."

Well, someone is liverish today. If I knew you desired to speak with me, I would have answered. I thought you wanted me silent.

"I do want you silent." Iris crossed the room, removed the panel, and took the hatbox out of its hiding place. She plopped down on the bed with it and untied the ribbon. Her stomach dropped as she lifted the deck of tarot cards, and her fingers shook as they gripped the braided hair. She secured the rope around the deck, then snatched up the matchbox beside the candles on her nightstand and placed her used cereal bowl on her knees.

She eyed the three-quarters-full water bottle beside her alarm clock as she took out a match. One strike, two strikes, three… The match ignited. She put the flame against the glossy purple box with green vines on it. The flame danced across the surface before going out. There wasn't a burn mark. Iris lit another one, and the same thing happened.

Are you quite finished? I could have told you it would not burn, but you wished me silent. Only the fate changer who controls the cards can destroy them.

Iris tossed the bowl, cards, matches on the bed and pressed her palms against her eyes. "What did you do to her? To Lauren? And how did that card—how did it fall out?"

I only did what you wanted me to—deep in the corners of your mind. Revenge. She abandoned you when you needed her most.

"Go away. Just go away. Leave me alone." She rubbed her eyes and slid the hatbox to her side. At touching the notebook, a sharp pain shocked her head like a lightning strike across her skull.

You shouldn't touch what isn't yours. Pick up the deck.

"No," Iris said, barely audible.

Not this again. I hate causing you pain, dear one.

"Don't call me that."

You hurt me. I thought we understood each other. Do as I wish, and there will be no pain.

Iris groaned in agony. It was as if her brain were being wrung out like a dishtowel. She was nauseous, so she picked up the wastepaper basket and leaned over it. *It's a tumor. I must have a tumor or something.* She heaved into the trash. Her throat was on fire. She grabbed the half-filled water bottle and chugged it down.

Another sharp pain hit her right temple and she winced. "*Stop.* Please."

Had enough, dear one?

"*Yes,*" she moaned.

The tarot cards. Pick them up.

The pain subsided and her stomach settled. Iris put down the trash can and picked up the deck. She needed help. No one would believe her if she told them what was happening to her. Or maybe they would. Especially after all the crazy stuff that went down with Aster. She had to tell Violet. Her sister would help.

Sit down! The voice sounded pissed. *I would never let you tell anyone about me. You do, I will force you to give them a bad fate.*

Iris sat back down on the bed and picked up the tarot cards.

Shuffle through them.

She flipped over a card at a time onto her turquoise comforter with the white irises on it. The images on the cards were blurry with the tears glossing her eyes. She had entered a nightmare and had no idea how to get out of it.

No, not that one.

Iris flipped another card.

That won't do, either.

And another.

Hmm… The Justice card. That could work. Touch it.

Iris decided not to fight it. How could she anyway? The woman was in her head. She knew her thoughts. She could hurt her family.

I'm pleased to see you've finally accepted that.

"You're ruining my life."

Nonsense. I'm helping you.

She touched the card with a queen wearing a red robe, sitting on a throne, and holding up a sword. Inky black moved across the green vines, consuming them. "Who gets this one?"

That worm. Perry.

Iris's head was floating. "What will it do to him?"

He harms others, so he shall suffer.

"You won't hurt or kill him, will you?"

No. An eye for an eye.

"If I give it to him, you'll leave me alone?"

Yes. I get tired and must rest. I am new to this body.

"All right." Iris wasn't too sure she should trust the woman or spirit or whatever she was. How did Iris know the spirit would keep her word? It was a spirit, after all. Was there even a code ethics for specters?

That's my dear. Tomorrow will be judgment day for Perry.

"Please stop calling me dear," Iris said.

There was no response from the voice. Blood trickled from Iris's nose. She touched the wetness with her fingertips and stared at the red stain on her skin. "Oh my God—" A guttural sob broke from her lips. "What are you *doing* to me?" She yanked out a few tissues from a box on her crowded nightstand. Holding her nose with the tissue, she leaned her head back. *Please…just leave me alone.*

When the silence lasted for more than ten minutes, Iris put the things back in the hatbox and returned it to its hiding place under the window seat.

Someone knocked on the bedroom door.

"Just a minute!" Iris held the tissue to her nose with one hand as she put the panel back in place with the other one, then she slipped the tarot card in the front pocket of her backpack. "Come in."

Violet eased open the door. "Hey, you okay?"

"Yes. Why?"

She stepped into the room. "I don't know. Could it be you're banging things around and your nose is bleeding?"

"I hit it looking for something." Iris removed the tissue and dabbed at her nose to see if it was still bloody.

"And what is that *smell*? Did you puke?"

"Yeah," Iris said, placing her hand on her stomach. "I must've eaten something bad today."

Violet looked as if she wasn't sure what to do or if she

should go. Actually, Iris wasn't sure, either.

Grasping her hands behind her back and brushing the carpet back and forth with the toe of her shoe, Violet definitely had something on her mind.

"What is it?" Iris asked. The expression on her sister's face concerned her. It was a cross between worry and begging. She was about to drag Iris into something. Usually, it was some cause. They'd participated in many before. From save the dolphins to recycling campaigns.

"Lauren," she said. "I'm worried about her. I know how she feels. It sucks being violated like that."

"Okay." Where was she going with this?

"Okay? That's it?" She walked across the room and sat on the window seat. "She wants to talk to you. To apologize and maybe get to be friends again."

Iris sighed, a long, drawn-out one. "When I needed her the most, she turned her back on me. She stood by and let them bully me so many times. I can't even—"

"She's not happy about it."

"I'm not happy about it. Who cares if she's not?" Iris glanced at the bloody tissue in her hand before dropping it in the wastebasket.

"She was scared."

"I was scared."

Violet huffed. "Will you stop doing that?"

Iris noticed the panel underneath where Violet was sitting hadn't been secured properly. Though her sister knew the hatbox was hidden in there, Iris worried she would get suspicious with the panel loose and ask Iris if she'd been messing with the hatbox.

"Doing what?" Iris sat at the edge of her bed, trying to keep her eyes from going to the panel.

"That repeating thing you're doing."

"Repeating thing?"

Violet let out an exasperated breath. "See, that. You keep repeating whatever I say."

The doorbell ringing downstairs muffled through the walls. "That must be Wade here to tutor me," Iris said, grateful to get Violet out of her room.

Violet stood when Iris did. "I feel like we got nowhere with this. Anyway, I think we should show some empathy and accept Lauren into our group. Carys agrees. And we're going to throw a huge Halloween party. No one needs Josh and his zombies or Marsha's crazy parties. Someone always gets hurt at them. Lauren isn't the only one who was tricked into taking damaging photographs, you know. If we all band together, they'll be outnumbered and they won't be able to hurt people anymore."

Iris hated Marsha's parties. Violet was right, bad things always happened at them.

"We only have a few weeks to plan the party," Violet said. "So are you in?"

Iris opened the door. "You seriously need a nomination for sainthood. If you can forgive her for doing terrible things to you, then I can try. Keyword being *try* here. I'm on decorations. And my zombies will definitely resemble Josh and company."

"That's all I ask," Violet said and hugged Iris from behind. "We can change the world, you and me."

"Seriously?" Iris chuckled. "We haven't said that in years."

"But it's true, right?" She bopped down the hall to her room.

"I doubt it," Iris muttered, watching her as she closed her bedroom door. How Violet had turned around from complete desperation to faithful hope was beyond Iris's comprehension. The meds and doc must be a great recipe. Maybe *she* should seek help from Violet's doctor. Because if it wasn't magic haunting her, then Iris was going certifiably insane. And if it was magic, she was determined to find a way to stop it. She suspected that hatbox had the clues she needed, but the voice wouldn't let her explore it.

Miri. The woman who had tested her and Violet to see if they were fate changers. She would know.

Iris waited to hear if the craggy voice would get mad at her. The only sound was the voice of her little sister, Daisy, and Wade coming from downstairs. The voice had said she needed rest, and the old bat probably wasn't listening to Iris's thoughts now. She rushed to her desk, wrote a quick note, and stuffed it into her backpack.

Chapter Eight

WADE

A brisk wind came off the ocean, carrying a scent of salty fish. No one was around. The only sound came from the boats rocking in the small waves and banging against the docks. Wade stuck his hands in his pockets and glanced over at Iris. She wrapped her arms around her body; he was sure her thin jean jacket didn't offer much warmth against the autumn night. Noticing her lip shiver slightly, he tugged his hands free and started to remove his leather coat.

Iris stopped.

Wade turned to face her. "What's wrong?"

The lights coming from the boathouse lit her face and made her eyes look like blue bottle glass. "You don't have to do that," she said. "My jacket is fine. Besides, you need yours." She smiled then. "I do appreciate the gesture, though."

"Will you just let me do this?" he said, removing it and draping it over her shoulders. She could be real stubborn sometimes. "I'm not trying to show ownership or anything.

When a guy offers his coat, it's about chivalry. Plus, my mom would bust my butt if I didn't. And you never want to get a Cuban woman angry."

"Way to stereotype your mom."

"I'm not."

She laughed. "Yes you are. Your mom is hardly ever mad. She's pretty reasonable. And impressive. A lawyer. Running for senate—"

He groaned, cutting her off. "All I wanted to do was show I cared and keep you warm."

"You didn't let me finish," she said. "I was going to say, *and* she raised a caring and awesome son." She lightly bumped her shoulder into him and smirked. "And a pretty handsome one at that."

He smiled at her compliment. "Okay, I get it. I shouldn't be so sensitive."

She lowered her head, watching her steps. "I like the sensitive types."

The wind blew Iris's hair around her face and she brushed it aside. Damn, she was beautiful. And pretty cool, when she wasn't breaking his heart. She out-ate him in dollar hot dogs at the school fair once. Could belch louder than him after drinking a Dr Pepper. Even bested him in chess too many times it would make his balls shrink to admit. And she was cute while doing it all.

They walked close together on the narrow decking, their fingers briefly brushing against each other. She jumped a little and quickly moved her hand away.

He wanted to hold her hand, but something kept him from making the play. Nerves? Uncertainty? There was a voice continuously looping in his head. Something his dad had always said. *Burn me once, shame on you. Burn me twice, shame on me.* Or was it fool me? Whatever it was, it made sense.

Could he trust her? That's what kept playing in his head. He hated feeling insecure when it came to Iris. To his once best friend.

Just then, she glanced at him. Her smile was dazzling, and that cute upturned nose with a dusting of freckles strangled his heart. All the memories. All the time they'd been best friends. They were all outweighed by the one time she had crushed him. Whatever the reason she did it or however good her intentions were, it still hurt.

They approached his grandfather's sailboat, and he offered his hand to help her onboard.

"Oh my gosh, Wade," she said as he stepped up after her. "It's beautiful. It looks brand new. You've done so much work on it."

He was proud of it. The recent paint and varnish had brought new life to it. "I only need a new sail and I can bring it out for a run. It's taking forever to raise the money, though."

"Won't your parents help you with some of the cost?"

He picked up the LED lantern and turned it on. "My mom doesn't like my sailing, and this is a surprise for my dad. I'm hoping it'll lift his spirits, you know. He used to sail with my papa when he was younger. I made this for him." He directed the lamp's light to the ramp he'd constructed. His dad had been paralyzed when a drunk driver crushed his Lexus.

"How is your dad doing?"

Wade lowered his arm, the light following his movement. "The locomotor training is working. He can stand and take a few steps now."

"That's wonderful."

"Yeah, we're hopeful. This way," he said, nodding toward the cabin.

She didn't move, giving him a curious eye.

"It's not what you think." He chuckled and stepped down into the cabin, putting the lamp on the table just as she landed off the bottom step.

"Oh wow, this is amazing. Something smells good. Were you cooking in here?"

He grinned as he watched her inspect the newly updated kitchenette and varnished cabinets. The cabin did turn out better than he thought it would. It was like the inside of one of those expensive campers he saw with his dad at a trade show once.

"A man gave me the appliances," he said. "His boat got it bad in the last hurricane. Carys did the upholstering and decorated the place."

She stopped at the table Wade had arranged with one of his mom's tablecloths and two full place settings of her china and silver. "You really outdid yourself."

"I thought it would be cool to start at the beginning. You know, how I used to cook for you all the time back when we were friends." He took the lighter out of the kitchen drawer and lit the tea lights in the middle of the table.

She gave the candles a suspicious look.

"And these aren't for romantic effect," he said. "We just need more light. Have a seat." Yeah, it totally looked romantic. He should've gone with paper plates, but he hadn't had the time to buy any.

"I'm so impressed," she said, sliding into the booth.

The oven was still warm, though he'd turned it off more than thirty minutes ago when he went to pick up Iris. He opened the oven door, removed the tray from within, and closed it with his knee. After he placed the tray on the side of the table, he scooted across the bench seat next to Iris.

She looked from the tray to Wade. "You made potato balls?"

"*Papas rellenas,*" he said.

"I know." She smiled. "I just like how you say that."

He chuckled. "Well, I hope that's okay," He removed the

tinfoil from a bowl full of salad on the table.

"Are you kidding?" She took the paper napkin from the etched floral plate and unfolded it. "I love them. I miss going to your house for dinner. Your grandmother taught you well."

"I'll tell her you said so the next time she calls." Wade spooned some salad onto a plate and set it in front of Iris, and then he scooped some onto a plate for himself.

After piling on a few fried balls filled with mashed potatoes and spicy beef, Iris took a crunchy bite, most of the insides escaping and plopping on her plate. "Delicious," she said, which came out somewhat incoherent with her mouth full.

When they were finished, Wade served flan and tea with cream.

Iris leaned back against the cushions. "I feel spoiled. Working at your uncle's restaurant is really paying off."

"Yeah, I enjoy it. I'm thinking of going to culinary school after graduation."

"It's really cool he uses your grandmother's recipes."

"It was hard getting them out of her. She'd take them to her grave if she could." Wade stretched back on the cushions behind him.

The boat rocked as they sat there, neither one speaking, the faint sound of the waves lapping against the boat's hull filling the silence. Wade adjusted on his seat, his fingers barely touching Iris's hand.

He was crazy to be so nervous around her. It was Iris. They'd known each other forever. Her leg brushed against his and excitement rushed through him. They stared at each other, and he fought back the urge to kiss her.

Friends. But I want to be more than that.

She had a way of making him fall. Like a bird with a broken wing, falling and spinning out of control. He thought about straightening to break the intense eye contact going on between them. It was like a magnetic field pulling them closer. He lowered his head, but before their lips met, her eyebrows crinkled and she straightened, moving away from him.

She clutched her head and groaned. Her breaths went heavy and she leaned back against the cushions.

Wade grabbed her wrists, trying to pull her hands away. "What is it?"

"Pain— Headache." She fell against him and he wrapped his arms around her.

"Can you move?" Wade didn't know how to help her. Adrenaline rushed through him. He had to do something.

She shook her head against his chest. *"No."* There was desperation in her tone.

"I'll call 911." He scanned the table for his cell phone and remembered he'd left it on the counter.

"No. No, I'm okay." She wiggled away from him. "It's gone."

"Has this happened before?" He didn't like this.

"No." She picked up her teacup, her hand shaking, and took a sip. "I was up late studying."

Was she hiding some illness from him? He'd never seen anyone get a sudden headache that went away as fast as it had started. It could be a brain aneurysm or something equally serious. Several years ago, his aunt had gotten one while watching her kids at a park and died on the spot. But he wouldn't say that to Iris. He wouldn't want to scare her.

Wade slid out of the booth. "I should get you home so you can rest."

"Let me help you clean up." She scooted to the other end of the seat and stood.

"It's no problem," he said. "There's no running water. I just have to toss it all in a container."

When he'd finished putting the used dishes and leftovers in the container, he made sure the propane was off and the cabin secured before walking with Iris back to his dad's car. She avoided eye contact with him the entire drive to her house, staring out the window. The only words spoken were him asking how she was every few minutes. With each of her answers that she was fine, he sensed her annoyance.

"I'm fine," she would say, just staring out at the street.

He pulled the car up to the curb. By the time he made it to the passenger side to help her out, she was already on the sidewalk.

"You know what the problem with today's youth is?" he asked, burying his hand in his pants pocket as he walked alongside her.

"You sound like my dad," she said. "I give. What's wrong with us?"

"Girls don't let guys open their doors for them."

She gave him a sidelong glance. "You're really into this chivalry thing, aren't you? Have you been watching some classic romance movies lately?"

"No. My dad used to open doors for my mom and give her his coat when she was cold." He kicked a rock on the sidewalk, and it skipped along until it settled in the grass. "He can't do that anymore. But I can. Maybe I'll start a trend. Before long, you'll have guys rushing to open doors for you."

"I'm not sure I could handle that." She laughed. "I'm perfectly capable of opening my own doors."

"I concede," he said. "I'll try not to open them for you."

She glanced at him again. "You give up too easily. If you're going to make a change, you can't be chased off by some opposition."

"Look at you using fancy words."

"Yep. I read the dictionary at night," she said.

"Well, that would definitely put you to sleep." He motioned for her to go up the steps before him.

At her door, before she went inside, she turned to face

him. "I had a great time. Thanks for making it so special."

"I hope you feel better." He backed away. "See you at school?"

She stood in the doorframe, what seemed to be a disappointed look on her face. "Okay."

He turned and bounded down the steps.

"Stop it." He thought he heard her say, but it was so quiet and sounded like a hiss.

He glanced back.

She was rubbing at her temples.

"Did you say something?" he asked.

"Um...no, sorry. Good night." She ducked inside and shut the door.

Wade sat in his dad's van. He wasn't sure what had just happened. Most of the night went great. They were making progress. What was up with the sudden headache? Was it real or did she fake it so she could end their date early?

Dammit. There it was again, the insecurity, questioning if he trusted her or not. He started the ignition and drove off.

Chapter Nine

IRIS

Across the table from Iris, Daisy ate her Cocoa Krispies, milk dribbling from the spoon and landing on the table. She was a mini Aster with her dark auburn hair and golden eyes. Looking at her made Iris miss her oldest sister. It wouldn't be long before Iris and Violet went off to college and Daisy would be alone. But Iris was sure Daisy would be fine. She acted thirty not fifteen, except when she was eating.

"Maybe you could make it all into your mouth," Iris said, taking a bite of her toast.

Daisy shoveled another spoonful of cereal into her mouth.

She is lacking in manners. My mother would have boxed my ears for eating in such a rush.

Your mother? Iris asked the voice, hoping to get clues as to who this spirit, curse, voice, or whatever was when she was alive—if she were ever that. Alive. Maybe she was a demon and has always been a curse.

You could just ask me, the voice taunted.

Daisy dipped her spoon into her bowl. "Where's Violet? How come she's not taking me to school today?"

"She had to open the shop before school for the new employee." With their mom gone, the twins were responsible for the family's flower shop. Iris took a sip of her orange juice. "So you're stuck with me."

Daisy rolled her eyes. "I was just wondering where she was. I don't feel *stuck* with you. Are you sick?"

"No. Why?"

"You have dark circles under your eyes and your face is paler than normal."

"It's nothing. I'm just stressed." Iris rolled her neck. The headaches had come and gone the last few days, and she kept losing track of time—small periods were black voids in her mind. Not being able to remember what she had done during her passing period between math and English yesterday concerned her.

Iris slid two notes over to Daisy she had written several days ago when the craggy voice was sleeping. One was to Miri and the other was to Daisy with instructions. She hoped Daisy would help her and that Miri would know a way to get rid of the curse Iris was sure had inflicted her.

What did you give her?

"That's your permission slip for your school trip," Iris said, giving Daisy the look the sisters would make around others that said, *Go along with me.*

Daisy stared at Iris for a few seconds before catching on. She opened the envelope with her name and read it. "Well, at least Mom didn't forget this. It did slip her mind to give me lunch money, though."

"I have some you can borrow until she gets back." Iris picked up her toast and finished the last bite, struggling to keep all thoughts off what was really in the note. "The other is a delivery for Mom. So hurry up. We'll swing by the boardwalk before school and you can run it in."

"Sure." Daisy stood and rushed off to get ready.

Iris hopped in the shower and got dressed.

I feel as if you are up to something. No thoughts. Your mind is a blank.

"I'm tired." Iris spoke to her reflection in the mirror over the bathroom sink, grabbing her toothbrush. "What happened yesterday? There's parts of the day I can't remember."

You fought with me. I warned you I would completely take over if you resisted me. You refused to give that boy his tarot card.

"Perry?" There was a sinking feeling in Iris's stomach. "What did you do?"

I gave him what he deserves. All shall show itself soon.

"What does that mean?" She dropped her toothbrush, and it clattered against the marble counter. *The justice card*, Iris recalled. How would he be judged? By his peers or teachers? Iris picked back up her toothbrush and scrubbed her teeth. She was so distracted that she brushed them until her gums were raw. After rinsing her mouth, she hurried downstairs. Daisy waited by the back door for her—backpack in hand and a concerned look on her face.

"Got everything?" she asked, picking up the Bug's keys.

"Of course," Daisy said. "Why does everyone treat me like a baby?"

"Because you will always be the baby." Iris yanked open the door.

The entire drive to the Ocean City boardwalk, Iris struggled to come up with small talk. "How're your friends?"

"You mean *friend*?" Daisy said, staring out the window. "Since I only have the one now that Abby told everyone that I ratted on her."

Abigail Massey. The bad girl of the ninth graders and Daisy's temporary friend. Her sister was in big trouble for partying and shoplifting with that brat and her friends. Abby had stolen the deposit for the floral shop while their mom was rescuing Violet from an attempted suicide.

Their mom almost had to close the shop because of it. All the result of Aster changing people's fates. And why Daisy feared tarot cards and refused to be tested to see if she was a fate changer. Iris couldn't blame Daisy for not wanting to know. The thought of having that power and the consequences that went with it was full-on scary.

Iris parked the Bug, positioning it so that she faced away from the boardwalk. Daisy popped open the door and briskly walked away.

She's an interesting girl. The voice sounded tired.

Iris strangled the stirring wheel. *Stay away from her.*

I had a younger sister. She was kind and frail like Daisy.

Just go away. If Iris could cut the woman out of her brain, she would.

Dark clouds moved across the morning sky. Rain sprinkled the windshield, and Iris watched as the water gathered and chased down the glass plane. The clock on the dash ticked away the minutes. On the seventeenth tick, Daisy opened the door and fell onto the seat.

"I got them," Daisy said, passing her the bag. "The drops for your anemia. The woman at the vitamin counter said to take a dropperful immediately. And that you should never go so long without them again. And don't take too much. It makes you sick."

What is this? The voice was angry. *I wasn't aware you had an illness... Ah, yes, there it is. So distraught you were when Aster changed your fate and broke the tie you had with that boy, you stopped eating. I, too, had a broken heart once.*

The woman's thoughts blaring in Iris's head was as annoying as being stuck on a radio station that played music you hated. Iris took the bottle out of the bag, unscrewed the top, and drank down a dropperful of the liquid inside. It tasted bitter and burned her tongue, but she hoped it would quiet the voice.

The voice rasped on, not aware of what Iris was up to. *I was desperate once. Just like you. Thought I could get my love back. Instead, I died a girl of fifteen with no love at my side. There's no hope. You will never have your Wade.* Tears stung the backs of Iris's eyes and she wasn't sure if it was her emotions or those of the old woman possessing her.

I am getting tired… The voice faded out.

Iris rubbed her temples. She almost felt sorry for the old woman. But if she had died young, why did she seem so old? Her voice sounded like a heavy smoker's. Maybe the curse caused it.

"Are you okay?" Daisy asked, struggling to pull out her seat belt. "We have to go. We're going to be late for the first bell."

Iris turned the ignition and pressed on the gas pedal. She drove the Bug in the direction of school, passing in and out of the shadows of trees lining the street. The clouds parted and released ribbons of sunlight that glistened across the wet asphalt. "What did Miri say?"

"She said to use the drops only twice a day, and only a dropperful." Daisy held onto the doorframe as Iris took a quick corner. "Any more and you could poison yourself. It will suppress the spirit for a few hours at best. She's looking for a way to get rid of it."

"Okay, good." She took another corner.

"You know, this is crazy. Are you sure you're possessed?"

"A hundred percent sure." Iris glanced over at her. "I touched Aster's tarot cards, and there was a cursed spirit it them. It went inside me and is using me for a sick game."

"What game?"

"She's trying to get even with people who I subconsciously

or knowingly want revenge on." Iris pulled to the curb in front of the school. "Get out here, so you won't be late. I'll go park. And don't worry. I won't let anything happen to you. I'll find a way to get rid of her."

"I hope so." Daisy sounded as uncertain as Iris felt. She switched her gaze from Iris to the window. Students rushed over the sidewalks heading for the school's entrance. The clouds darkened the sky again and the wind picked up, tossing orange, yellow, and red leaves onto the lawn below.

"Listen," Iris said, drawing Daisy's attention from the window. "Don't say anything to Violet. She's been doing so well. I don't want this to mess with her head, you know?"

"Yeah, I agree." Daisy opened the door and before getting out, she leaned over and hugged Iris. "Please be careful."

"I will." Before Daisy closed the door, Iris said, "Maybe you should stay at Amber's house until this blows over."

"But what about you?"

"I'll be fine, and I'll feel better knowing you're safe."

"Okay." She shut the door and jogged up the sidewalk toward the entrance doors. Out of all the sisters, Iris would have to say Daisy was the prettiest, smartest, and kindest of them all. Gram was always saying that Daisy had the look of a young Audrey Hepburn with red hair and the brains of Einstein.

Rain clapped the windshield as Iris waited until Daisy joined her friend, Amber, by the bike rack, tugging her hoodie over her head to shield her from the downpour. Whatever it took, Iris was determined to protect her sisters.

The school hallways were buzzing with huddled groups gossiping loud enough for Iris to catch bits of their conversation.

"Did you see that?"

"They took Perry out in handcuffs."

"What did he do?"

"He broke into the game store."

"Stole tons of games and a game console."

"I heard he shot a police officer."

What? Iris almost tripped herself, but she spotted Wade and Dena and pushed forward. *You said no one would get hurt.*

There was no answer.

"He didn't shoot anyone," Wade was saying to Dena when Iris approached them. "Man, rumors can get out of hand around here. Idiots. Don't they have better things to talk about?"

"Hi," Iris said, relieved to hear Perry hadn't killed anyone. The halls smelled of cleaner with a mix of whatever the cafeteria workers were baking for lunch. She wasn't sure if it were the combination of scents or Perry's fate making her stomach turn.

"Hey," Wade responded. "You feeling better today?"

"Yes. Why?"

Wade gave her a curious look. "You threw up at lunch yesterday."

I did? She hadn't remembered that. It must've happened when the spirit had snatched her body. What else had happened? Iris wasn't sure she wanted to know. Goose bumps rose on her arms at the thought. She rubbed them. When her gaze went back to Wade, he was watching her suspiciously.

"It was probably something I ate," she said. "I feel fine today."

"That's good," Wade said, his eyes still scrutinizing her.

Dena glanced from Wade to Iris. "You two are the most awkward friends I've ever met. Wait. That's because you're not *friends*. You're lovers. When are you going to accept that?"

"We're not awkward," Iris muttered at the same time Wade said, "We're not lovers."

Wade's answer disappointed Iris, but it was silly for her to feel that way. They weren't lovers. No matter how much she wanted them to be, she knew he might never get there.

"But we're working on it," he said.

Working on it? His words caused tingles to ignite in her stomach. All thoughts of her sucky life vanished. There was hope. *He's working on it.*

Violet rushed up to them. "Hi guys. Are we on for after school? I have a group coming over to start on the props for the Halloween party. I'm thinking a haunted house between the garage apartment and the house. Sam at the rental place Mom uses for events is letting us borrow an old tent he has."

The passing bell rang.

"I'll be there," Wade said. "Catch you later." He sauntered off without Iris. Their classes were in the same hall, and he used to walk with her to hers.

A chill rushed up her spine. Was he mad at her? Had she done something yesterday to piss him off? But she didn't have any idea what happened, and she had a horrible feeling it was something her spirit guest had done.

Chapter Ten

WADE

Stubborn strands of reddish-blond hair kept falling across Iris's cheek as she painted a graveyard on a large wall constructed from several pieces of cardboard. The light breeze swirled the fall leaves around the carport, and the scent of paint and turpentine mingled with the briny smell of the ocean.

She looked peacefully lost in her painting. Wade used to be her other escape. Those easy days, when they'd laugh and play for hours, were gone. He so wanted them back.

Iris's artwork looked lifelike, and she had a skill at making the gravestones seem three-dimensional. The gore and blood she painted on the creatures were frightening. Wade bet her paintings would freak out anyone who walked through the haunted house in the dark.

Carys sat on the step stool next to where Wade knelt as he constructed a coffin. She was Cuban like Wade. There weren't many in the area, so their mothers became close friends when Wade's family moved to Ocean City.

Tying her dark, curly hair into a ponytail, Carys noticed him watching Iris. "How's it going?"

"Good." He pounded a nail into the wood.

She had a look on her face as if she'd been hit with his hammer.

"What's up?" He sat back on his heels, squinting against the sun.

She rubbed her nose. "If you did something, and you know admitting it would ruin a friendship, would you tell that person? I mean, it would totally end a relationship. And possibly get physical."

"Would telling that someone change things?" he asked.

"No." She frowned. "They could never go back to the way it was before the thing that happened…happened."

He couldn't image Carys hurting someone. She was always rescuing those in need. Because of her, his dad was alive. The accident that had paralyzed him had happened after an event for his mother's first run for senate. Her car was following behind his when the drunk driver T-boned his Lexus. When Wade saw her at the hospital that night, her sleeves were stained with his father's blood. She had used her sweater to stop the bleeding from a gash in his chest. Never leaving his side, she kept him awake until the paramedics arrived.

Her hopeful eyes on him made him want to protect her.

"Is that person sorry for what they did?" he asked.

"Yes, *so* sorry. Wished it never happened."

"I wouldn't say anything," he said. "Just let it go."

"You sure?"

Wade grabbed another nail. "Yeah. Don't sweat it."

"Thanks. I'll try." She pushed herself up from the stool and walked off.

He was tired of everyone fighting and holding grudges about stupid shit. Worse things were happening in the world. They could all live in a war zone or be paralyzed in a car accident. Wade was all too familiar with the latter. It had turned his life upside down.

The nail wobbled a little when he slammed the hammer down on it. Across the way, Iris studied her work, the tip of her paintbrush handle against her lip. She nodded as if to approve of what she'd created so far.

He could watch Iris paint for hours. Her shirt slipping with the stroke of the paintbrush in her hand, exposing just a bit of her shoulder. Concentrating, she'd pull her bottom lip between her teeth. When she straightened and arched her back during breaks, her butt rose slightly in those tight jeans. She'd worn them so many times a hole had formed just under her right back pocket. Her fingers brushed those loose strands of hair from her cheek as if she were playing a musical instrument.

But there was something off about her. She seemed distracted lately. The dark circles under her eyes concerned him. Was she sick or just unable to sleep at night? And if she was restless, was it because of him or because her mom and Grams were gone?

It was a warm Saturday, and the sun heated the back of his neck as he worked on his assignment. He glanced around at the others, anything to get his mind off Iris.

Violet practiced the makeup she planned for the event, turning Dena, who sat on the porch steps with her, into a zombie. Carys knelt on a tarp in the middle of the driveway and continued working with some sort of goop. She formed it to look like intestines and brains. Lauren was struggling to make her own creepy body parts.

The girls tried hard to keep Lauren's mind off the cyberbullying she'd suffered. Violet's empathy for others impressed Wade. He was like that—always defending the underdogs. He learned that from his mother. She fought hard for minorities, and he imagined Violet would make a great humanitarian after graduation.

Wade removed the last nail he had in the empty sour cream container beside him and hammered it into the coffin he was constructing. He picked up the tub and headed for the garage where Violet had said all her grandfather's tools were. He searched the worktable and shelves for nails.

Someone came in, and he glanced over his shoulder in the direction of the noise. Iris walked like a gazelle over to him, opened the second drawer from the top on the side of the worktable, took out a box of nails, and handed it to him.

She leaned against the worktable and gave him a sidelong glance. "Why are you mad at me?"

He shook the box, rattling the contents to see how full it was. "You don't remember?"

"So you *are* mad at me."

"Yep." He couldn't believe she was going to play dumb. "I have a coffin that needs nailing."

She laughed. "That sounds so wrong."

Damn, her laugh was cute.

He was not going to let her make him forget the other day. The drawer she left open squealed as he shut it before heading for the door.

"That's it?" she said, following him. "You're not going to tell me?"

He paused, his back still turned to her. "You handed something to Perry. I asked about it. You said I was jealous and a heathen. Remember now? And why were you talking like that?"

It was quiet behind him, so he glanced over his shoulder at her. She bit the corner of her mouth, a worry on her face.

"Obviously I was joking around," she said. "And I gave Perry something he dropped in class. That was all. I'm sorry. If I knew you didn't get it, I would have added the aside."

He whirled around. "The aside?"

"Yeah, you know, *JK*."

"It didn't seem like a joke."

She heaved a sigh. "What are we doing?"

He shrugged. "I don't know. What *are* we doing?"

"Don't do that."

"What?"

"Turn my question on me," she said. "I thought we were trying to make it work."

Wade's gut clenched at the hurt in her eyes. It just occurred to her what he already knew. There was no going back. His messed-up head would always wonder if she was into him or not. Handing something to Perry. Laughing at another guy's joke. It would be there. An uneasiness.

Yeah, he was jealous.

No. Not that.

Insecure. That's what he was. He hated being that guy. She made him that guy.

"Are you ending things?" She wringed her hands. "We've been friends for years."

He let out a heavy breath. Was he?

Tears gathered on her bottom eyelids as she waited for him to answer, and he hated seeing her upset. His eyes locked on hers. "I don't want to end things, but should it be this difficult?"

"I just haven't been myself. I want this to work." She grabbed his shirt. "This can work. You're my best friend. I love you. I mean…you know…I love you as more than a friend."

The words.

The ones he longed to hear when she broke things off with him.

Needed to hear.

He wasn't ready to say them to her now. His mind held him back. He'd said them before, and the next day she was with Josh.

"Please, Wade." Tears tumbled down her cheeks. "Please forgive me. I can't tell you what happened, but I didn't mean to hurt you." She grasped his arms and gazed up at him, her hair sliding back and falling down her back, her shirt slipping off her shoulder again.

He leaned forward, lowering his head, wanting desperately to kiss her, but he couldn't. Instead, he rested his forehead against hers. "I want to. God, do I want to forgive you. But it's so hard. I'm trying, Iris. Really, I am. You just have to be patient with me."

"I can wait," she said. "I'm not going anywhere—"

"I think Iris said there were more drop cloths in the garage," Dena was saying, a little too loudly. Was Dena warning him that someone was coming?

Wade and Iris pulled away from each other and stepped behind the garage door.

"Why are you shouting?" Carys whispered. They were on the other side of the door.

Iris glanced up at him with a questioning look.

Wade shrugged.

"So no one will suspect we're doing something other than looking for drop clothes," Dena whispered.

"You're acting strange," Carys said. "There's nothing we can do about it now. It's over. Why don't you just forget about it? "

Iris made to step out from behind the door, but what Dena said next stopped her. "Because if anyone finds out about this, Violet will hate me."

"It's not your fault," Carys said. "Violet willingly took that selfie with you."

Wade peered through the crack between the door and the wall. Dena paced around Carys. "Maybe if she wasn't drunk, she wouldn't have taken it with me. And if I hadn't accidentally sent it to you instead of Violet, Marsha wouldn't have found it on your phone."

Iris stomped out of their hiding place. Wade reached for her hand to stop her, but she snatched it away.

Dena and Carys looked like they'd just been struck by paintballs.

Iris's wide eyes darted back and forth from Dena to Carys. "It was you? Hell no, you aren't going to tell her. She'd break again. I can't…" She shook her head, tears dropping on her cheeks. "I just…can't." She ran off for the steps leading to the beach.

Before running after her, Wade gave them both a pointed look. "I can't believe you two," he said. "Iris!" he called and bounded down the deck steps after her. "Iris! Stop!"

She did and looked out at the ocean.

Wade struggled through the sand, came up behind her, wrapping his arms around her and pressing his cheek to hers. "Hey, you know Dena and Carys. They didn't mean for this shit to happen."

"Did you know about it?" she asked, and he could barely hear her over the waves crashing against the shore.

"No," he said. "But I know Dena, and she loves Violet. She would never willingly hurt her. And you know that, too."

"I know." She took a deep breath and exhaled it slowly. "When will all this crazy stuff just go away? I want it to be like it was. Before Aster…" She wiped her cheeks with the heel of her palm.

"Before Aster what?"

She didn't answer right off, sniffling as she slipped her hands over his arms around her. "Before she left."

"We're getting older," he said, realizing he had his arms around Iris and it felt good. "Soon we'll all be off to college, and nothing will ever be the same again. That's life. It's always changing."

She leaned her head back against his shoulder. "I hate

change."

He laughed. "So do I."

She stared straight ahead, focusing on the waves. "I wish we could be like the ocean; it seems like it never changes."

"But it does," he said. "We just don't notice it."

And they stood there, him holding her, her squeezing his arms, their breaths rolling in and out like the waves, calming at the same time they were crashing.

When would he let go of his fear? He wanted to shout. Could they ever get back to normal?

Chapter Eleven

Nearly an hour had passed as Iris rifled through the hatbox, examining every piece of paper and each page in the several notebooks. Some were in Romanian written by Dika Froggatt, a great, great aunt of hers or something like that. She was also a fate changer, whose notes helped Aster remove the curse from her boyfriend, Reese.

Iris worried there was something in those foreign words that could help her. But luckily, she found a notebook in the stack that translated the pages to English. It would have been nice if she'd found it sooner and hadn't wasted her time on the other stuff. She'd taken the drops and wasn't sure how much longer she had until the haunting voice returned.

She tossed the notebook aside. "This sucks."

On the floor across from her, Daisy glanced up from a book she was reading. "This one's interesting. It's from Miri's family." She turned the book for Iris to read and pointed out a paragraph. "Did you know fate changers are a certain kind of witch? It talks about the Van Buren curse. That's Reese's family. Our family is tied to theirs by it. Only we can reverse the curses for them, but when we do, the curse goes to our family. Usually, a fate changer can change a fate without consequences, but because we're cursed, any fate we change, Van Buren or not, inflicts our family."

"So that's why Aster was hitting us with bad fates," Iris said, taking the book from her. "What else is in here?"

"Read that last paragraph." Daisy adjusted to sit pretzel-style. "It says that the curse's spirit is from that girl who made the curse in the first place. She was a witch. Her name is Crina. We're descended from her. Only a fate changer can get rid of her."

"Does it say how to do that?" Iris turned the page to read the next paragraph.

"Go down a little farther," Daisy said.

"A fate changer must capture the cursed spirit using her tarot deck," Iris read. "Well, that's vague. We need a fate changer. We need Aster."

Daisy started putting all the notebooks and scraps of paper back into the hatbox. "You keep the tarot cards so Crina doesn't suspect anything."

"So we're calling the spirit bitch by her name?" That sounded so wrong. Iris wasn't sure why she said it. Maybe to make light of what was going on or because she was scared, but it fell flat on Daisy, her face holding no emotions.

"I'm going to take this to my room and study everything. Maybe I can find a way to get rid of the *spirit bitch*." A smile hinted on Daisy's lips.

Iris laughed, but it wasn't a fun kind of laugh. It was part grateful at Daisy's response and part frustrated at the situation. "Sounds good," she said.

"I'd better go before she returns and finds out what we're up to," Daisy said, putting the top on the hatbox. "I'm going to take them to Amber's house. I'll bring it to Miri. Maybe she can help me decipher this stuff. Good thing drinking those drops keeps whatever you do from Crina. This entire thing is scary."

Iris stood with Daisy. "Wait. Did you tell Amber about all this?"

"Yeah, but she thinks it's just a game or something." Daisy crossed the room. "She won't tell anyone, and even if she does, no one would believe her."

"It's happening to me, and I hardly believe it myself." Another nervous laugh slipped from Iris.

Daisy rested her hand on the doorknob. "If we need a fate changer, we'd better come up with a plan on how to get Aster to come home."

"I was thinking about that, too. We'll have to call Aster the next break I get from Crina."

"Okay. Well, stay safe," Daisy said, opening the door.

"You, too."

Iris spread out on her stomach across her bed and tried to clear her mind of all thoughts. Having an intruder in her brain made her feel violated. Her intimate moments not her own.

She rested her chin on her crossed arms. When she was alone like this, the voice quiet in her head, she thought about things. Things she wished she could forget. Like, why Dena and Violet had to take a selfie without their shirts on while they were kissing. Or how did Dena mix up the cell phone numbers and send that photo to Carys instead of Violet? And how had Marsha Simmons gotten it? Iris was determined to find out.

Her phone vibrated beside her on the mattress. She glanced at the caller ID. It was Carys again. The girl wouldn't give up, calling constantly since yesterday.

Tweedledum and Tweedledee. Regardless of how silly their mistake, a mistake they did make.

"If you're so ancient, then how do you know *Alice in Wonderland* characters?"

I watch. I learn. You believe you can fool me, but you fail. I know you drink Mugwort and Mullein to keep me out. It's only a matter of time before I develop a resistance to it.

"I don't know what you're talking about." Iris sat up. "The drops are only vitamins."

Shall I show you what I have been working on during the dark hours?

Iris slipped off the bed to her feet. And it wasn't by her own will. Crina had made her do it.

I am getting stronger, wouldn't you say?

"Please leave me alone," Iris pleaded, struggling to move.

Where are the cards?

Iris glanced across the room. "On the window seat."

Crina released her, and Iris sat on the bed. *Go get them.*

"What are you going to do this time?"

Not telling. You cannot be trusted. Get the cards or I'll have you do something horrible. Like slit your wrists.

"What?" Iris's stomach clenched. Was that her thought or Crina's? The spirit's voice sounded less craggy. Iris was confusing the voices in her head. Maybe Crina wasn't a spirit and Iris was just going insane. No one really knows when they're crazy. But she kept reminding herself it was the curse. That fate changing existed. Driving it home so that she wouldn't lose herself to whatever—whoever—possessed her. To Crina.

If Crina could make her stand, she could make Iris do any number of things to herself. Make her cut her wrists. She went over and picked up the tarot deck, feeling beaten.

Let's see what we have to work with. We'll need two cards.

The market was packed. It was like Iris was one of those ghosts in *A Christmas Carol*—a bystander to past events. Crina and her younger sister, Della, strolled down the narrow aisle lined with shabby stands on each side. Vendors squawked out their offerings. Everything from fruits, nuts, and dried dates to fine hair combs, tools, and linens were up for sale.

The streets were dusty and a slight urine aroma hung in the air. No one seemed to notice the smell as Iris had. She wished she could make Crina plug her nose.

Crina searched the crowd. Armand never missed a market day. Not many did. She hadn't seen him in nearly a week. They went from meeting in the meadow every afternoon for a month to not seeing each other at all. She couldn't help but worry. Surely he could find a few hours away from his visiting cousins.

"The heat is unbearable this morning." Della patted her chest with a hanky. "Who do you search for, sister?"

Crina gave her a sidelong glance. "You know who I seek."

"No one has seen the Van Burens for nearly a week," Della said. "I hear Phillip Van Buren will marry his visiting cousin. It is said her face resembles a horse. Poor Phillip. Such a sacrifice. The cost of being an heir. I suppose there will be a grand festival should that happen. The Van Burens are always so generous to us lowly villagers when they have something to celebrate."

Crina was now glaring at her sister, her chattering grinding on her nerves. Pride burned in Crina's chest. She didn't think of herself as lower than Armand. "Soon I will be in America and far away from this place. In America there are no counts or kings. Everyone is equal."

"You are a fool to think Armand would leave with you." Della stopped at a stand with barrels of nuts.

Crina took Della's elbow and pulled her away from the stand. "Be careful what you say," she hissed. "He loves me.

You shall see. We will be gone from here soon."

"I hope so. For yours and your baby's sake."

Crina's eyes widened, and her hand went to her belly. She didn't have a baby bump as far as Iris could tell, but then again, the layers of her skirt could easily hide one.

"How did you know?"

Della smiled. "We share a bed. You are my sister. I know well your changes. I do hope your Van Buren marries you. I doubt that he will. There is still time, though. You could bed with Tomas. Say it is his child. He would take good care of you."

Crina's gaze went to a goofy-looking man, tall and lanky with large ears and curly dark hair, selling animal skins. "I cannot imagine a life with him. I'd rather die."

Some sort of excitement broke out in the crowd. People rushed around, whispering among one another. The movement was like a charging stampede coming for them.

A short woman with a crooked back and salt-and-pepper hair stopped in front of Crina and Della. "Did you hear? Such horrible news. The Van Buren heir was thrown from his horse. He is dead." She rushed off to tell someone else the news.

Crina stumbled and Della grasped her arm, helping Crina to stay upright. "What is wrong? It's Phillip not Armand."

"Armand." Crina's voice sounded dry and painful, and she grabbed her stomach. "Now the heir. He will never leave with me."

Nausea burned Iris's throat as darkness choked out the images of Crina, Della, and the market.

It was another warm day for October. It almost felt like spring. Fall decorations adorned the school windows and doors. The courtyard was crowded with students eating outside to enjoy the last of the warm days before the predicted cold front moved in.

Iris crossed the yard to Wade. Dena, Violet, and Carys were with him. He stood as she approached.

"You doing okay?" he asked, his brow furrowed with concern.

"You keep asking me that. I'm great," she said. She was anything but great. Her vision blackened at the edges. Crina was up to something. An intense pressure squeezed Iris's mind, pushing her back into the darkness. It was like watching her friends through a fogged mirror.

Iris glanced at the others. Dena and Carys avoided making eye contact with her. Rightfully so, since they had almost killed her sister with their dumb mistake.

Violet must've noticed their uneasiness. "Did I miss something? What's going on?"

"Nothing," Crina-as-Iris said. "But I thought it would be fun to have a tarot card drinking game at the party."

Dena turned her head in Iris's direction. "I love that idea."

"Iris, can I have a word with you? In private." Violet stepped away from the group and Iris followed her. When they were out of earshot, she turned to face Iris. "We are not having tarot readings at the party."

"Why not?" Crina-as-Iris crossed her arms.

Violet glared at her. "You know why not."

Chirping birds overhead competed with the loud voices in the courtyard.

"Neither one of us can change fates. It's perfectly safe."

"Why do you want to do this?" Violet gave her a questioning look. "I don't get it."

"Well, I found out that Josh is having a haunted house at his Halloween party, too." Iris searched the courtyard, making sure Josh's spies weren't nearby. "You know everyone is going to go to his party, not ours. So I started a rumor that we were having a new drinking game."

"Exactly how is this drinking game going to work?" Violet huffed.

"Those in the game take turns flipping over cards until someone ends up with the Death one or whichever other ones we choose to make wild. That person then has to drink. Simple as that."

No, no, no, no! Iris wanted to scream at Violet. *Please don't agree to it.*

"I'm not sure I like this idea," Violet said.

Oh good. Iris should've trusted Violet would never do something involving tarot cards, or binge drinking for that matter.

Crina-as-Iris exaggerated a pout. "Come on. We can't change fates with them like Aster. Nothing will happen."

Violet glanced around as if the answer were in the wind or something. "All right. If you think it will attract more people to our party."

Violet, no!

"Yep. Here, look at the flier I made." Crina-as-Iris reached into her backpack and pulled one out.

When did you draw that?

You were in some sort of trance while I used your skill, Crina answered her.

Crina had made Iris create a Victorian carnival with a tarot reader and partygoers dressed in the period's clothes drinking from red cups. In the background was a creepy haunted house.

Violet took the paper from her and studied it.

Dena came over and looked over Violet's shoulder. "That is some serious talent. It looks like a fun carnival."

"Thanks," Crina-as-Iris said, pulling out one of the tarot cards and holding it out to Dena. "Here's what the cards look like."

No! Iris shouted. *What are you doing? Don't give that to her.*

Hush, Crina hissed. *I am in control.*

Dena took the card. "Ouch."

Iris watched in horror as the vines on the back of the card went from black to green.

"What's wrong?" Violet gave Dena a worried look.

"Nothing. Just some intense static," she said. "This is a cool picture. The Hanged Man card." The image on the card was of a man hanging upside down by his feet. He looked like he was straight out of a Shakespearean play with red tights and a flouncy blue shirt.

What does that card do? Iris asked Crina.

It is time Violet knows what Dena did. Time for Dena to be caught. Accept responsibility for her actions.

Stop it. Iris pushed to take control of herself. *You think you're helping me, but you're not.*

I do not wish to help you, Crina responded. *I merely want to play the game. I cannot stop until the ultimate price is paid.*

What ultimate price? What are you planning?

Hush, Crina warned. *The other girl approaches.*

Carys stopped at Iris's side. "Wow, those fliers are beautiful."

"We're doing a tarot card drinking game. See," Crina-as-Iris said and handed her a card.

Grasping the card, Carys flinched. "Your bag must carry static or something. The card shocked me."

Violet's stare met Iris's gaze, a suspicious look on her face.

"The High Priestess," Carys said, holding up the card for everyone to see. "I love these. It's such a great idea." She handed the card back to Iris and walked off for their picnic table. "Come on, guys. Let's eat so we can pass out the fliers before lunch break is over."

Why did you give her that one? Iris felt defeated.

Crina cackled in her head. *She will know loss. Others will mistrust her.*

Are they all evil? Why? Iris wanted to cry, but she wanted to keep Crina distracted more. Her fingers inched for the bottle Miri had given her.

All the cards you touch and give to someone are cursed. So that means the reverse, or rather, the bad side of the card is given as a fate to your victims.

They're not my victims. They're yours. Iris grasped the bottle, quickly undid the top, and doused her tongue with a dropperful.

Sneaky. Sneaky. I am impressed. But it was my error. I should have hidden that bottle. You hurt my feelings, Iris. Haven't I helped you with grades, especially in the sciences? If you try to stop what I have put into motion, I will kill Violet. Do not try me. I will be back.

Kill Violet? Tears stung Iris's eyes. How could she continue? Violet was in danger. Everyone was in danger. She tried to swallow, but it was like there was cotton stuffed in her throat. She wanted this to end. She needed this to end. Her heart hammered against her chest. She had never felt so helpless before.

But she wasn't helpless.

She would fight. First thing, she had to hide the drops.

Her fingers shook as she fumbled to return the dropper to the bottle, almost spilling the liquid inside as she twisted the cap closed. Iris couldn't stop fighting. If she did, Violet would be lost and so would anyone else in Crina's path.

Bit by bit, Iris could feel herself gaining control of her body, but it was too slow. The others had passed out the fliers and were heading for their next classes. Iris texted Daisy before reaching her classroom, asking her to meet in the bathroom during their next passing period. Daisy could hide the drops for her. And hopefully Miri and Daisy had found a way to get rid of Crina.

Chapter Twelve

WADE

Wade pounded on the front door of the Laynes' house. It was a perfect afternoon, and there was no school today to allow for teacher conferences. Iris had texted him that her dad got great reviews back from all her teachers. His tutoring had paid off.

Mr. Layne opened the door. His dark hair was grayer since the last time Wade had seen him. He'd forgotten Iris said her father was down from Baltimore to keep an eye on the girls while their mom and gram were out of town. Iris had told Wade once that Mr. Layne's job was flexible. Benefits of working for his new wife.

"Hey, Wade, good to see you."

"Hello, sir. I'm here to pick up Iris."

"Yes, she mentioned you two were going out to celebrate," Mr. Layne said. "I'm quite pleased with her progress. Her science teacher said she's done a one-eighty with her tests. Aced every one so far." He pulled out an envelope. "Iris said you didn't want to be paid, but I'm insisting you take this."

"I can't do that," Wade said.

Mr. Layne never backed down. "Take it or I'll just go to the trouble of getting it to your mom so she can put it in your account."

There was no winning that battle.

"Besides," Mr. Layne added, "I hope you'll take me out on that boat of yours sometime."

Wade accepted the envelope. "Okay, thanks."

Mr. Layne stepped aside. "Go on in. I have to meet with Violet's teachers."

"Thank you," Wade said, passing him as he entered.

"See you later." Mr. Layne closed the door behind him.

The house was messier than Wade was used to seeing. The flowers in the vases around the living room were wilted, blooms bowing over their stems. There wasn't the scent of Gram Froggatt's baking in the air as usual. All definite signs that Iris's mom and gram were gone.

Iris pounded down the stairs, wearing jeans and a pullover hoodie. "Ready? Let's go," she said.

She was at the front door before he had a chance to register her presence.

"What's your hurry?" He trailed after her.

"I need to be back in a few hours." She skipped down the porch steps.

He closed the door and picked up the two helmets he had placed there before knocking on the door earlier. "You going to lock up?"

"Oh, I almost forgot." Darting back up the steps, she retrieved her keys from the front pocket of her jeans and locked the door.

"You don't have to rush," he said. "I'll have you back in a few hours. I promise."

"Sorry. I just have a project due tomorrow."

"Safety first," he said and slipped a helmet on her head.

She looked cute in the helmet, buckling it as she headed for his motorcycle. "Where are we going?"

Wade put on his helmet and straddled the bike. "To the marina."

She got on behind him and wrapped her arms around his waist, her thighs squeezing against his. Her touch always excited him.

When he steered the motorcycle into the parking lot of the marina, Violet, Dena, and Carys waited by Dena's Ford Focus. He parked and waited for Iris to get off before unsaddling the bike.

She removed her helmet. "I thought we were going to be alone."

"It's a special day." He opened the seat and put his and her helmets inside.

"Special? How?"

"You'll see," he said, crossing the parking lot to the others.

After saying their hellos, the group trekked over the docks until the second-to-last row where Wade's boat was kept in a slip. After they were all on the boat with life jackets secured, Wade motioned for Dena to untie it from the dock while he turned on the motor. The others found seats around the deck.

"So we're actually taking it out?" Iris said, standing beside Wade in the cockpit.

"Yep." He steered it through the marina to the open ocean, only having to avoid a few boats on his way. The harbor was nearly empty, with it being a workday.

Iris adjusted her feet to stay balanced with the rocking of the boat. "This will take longer than two hours."

"We're just going to head out a little ways for the big reveal," he said.

"Is the reveal that the boat won't sink?" Iris laughed.

He flashed a smile at her. "Funny."

The farther the sailboat moved away from the marina, the more excited Wade got. He couldn't believe that the boat was almost ready. He spent so much time with Dena and Carys fixing it up. This first run was for Iris. For the big reveal.

When he'd picked a perfect spot, he turned off the motor and looked over at her. "Want to take the helm?"

Wade and Dena rushed around hoisting the main sail. Next, they raised the jib. Carys and Violet clapped and whistled. Wade glanced back to see Iris's reaction. She squeezed the wheel tight, her hair whipping around her head as she looked up, her mouth wide. On the main sail was a dragon Iris had painted for him. The maker had copied the image and transferred it to the sail.

"What do you think?" Wade yelled over the wind.

Iris held her hair away from her face. Her expression excited Wade. "I love it!" she shouted over the crashing of the waves. The wind was perfect—not too weak and not too strong—and the boat went out for a bit before Wade brought it back to shore. After the sails were lowered and secured, he turned on the motor and maneuvered it to its place in the marina.

Dena and Wade went about tying the boat to the dock. Wade snuck glimpses of Iris as she took off her life jacket. Her back arched and her breasts pushed up, turning Wade on.

You're only torturing yourself, Diaz. He shook his head and finished off the knot he was tying.

A rope hit him in the face.

"Pay attention," Dena said, towing the rope back to her.

"I was," Wade said, grabbing the other end.

Dena shot him a knowing smile. "Not the kind of attention I meant."

When the boat was secured, Dena urged everyone into the cabin, where she opened a bottle of champagne and poured it into five clear plastic cups.

The last time Dena and he had champagne, they were

celebrating her coming out. Dena's parents weren't too pleased with her admission about her preference for girls. Her mother cried and her dad gave her the silent treatment. It wasn't until Dena's heart condition knocked her on her ass that they came around. After her surgery to fix a faulty valve, Dena's parents told her they only wished her happiness.

"To Wade," Dena said, holding up her cup, "congratulations on finishing this boat."

"Congratulations," Violet and Carys said in unison.

Iris rose her cup. "It looks amazing. Cheers."

"That sail is beautiful," Carys said and slipped into the booth. "It's from the painting Iris gave you, right? At a birthday or something?"

Violet and Dena scooted in next to Carys.

"Yeah, she gave it to me on my thirteenth birthday." Wade leaned against the counter and took a sip of the cheap champagne.

Iris leaned close enough to Wade that he could smell her floral shampoo. "You are so talented," she whispered, her breath tickling his ear and sending a spark through his body. He wished they were alone. He had an intense urge to kiss her.

He swallowed a big swig of bubbly. "Look who's talking. You have mad painting skills."

"So when are you taking your dad out?" she asked.

"Halloween morning. He'll be back this week sometime."

"Oh," she said. "What about the haunted house? We were going to set up that day."

"Don't worry." He brushed her hair away from her cheek and quickly brought his hand back.

She leaned away from him, a startled look on her face.

Why did I do that?

It was as if he were on autopilot. There was no thought behind it. "We're going early in the morning," he said, looking down at his cup. Bubbles popped in the golden liquid. "I'll be over in plenty of time to help out."

"Wade," she said so quietly the others couldn't hear her over their own conversation.

He looked at her.

She touched his arm. "You don't have to be afraid of me. I'm still Iris. I just made a mistake. I won't hurt you again." And then she mouthed, *I'm sorry*.

He wished he could forget, but he hadn't thought she would hurt him the first time. It was that fact that kept him from giving them another chance.

"Let's see the pictures of the sail," Violet said to Carys, causing Iris to break her gaze on Wade.

Carys slid her phone across the table. "I took a bunch. Tap All Photos so you can choose which ones you want to view."

Violet dragged her finger across the phone, scanning the pictures. She tapped one. "Oh gosh, this look on my face is horrible. Please delete that one."

"I don't delete pictures," Carys said. "They're memories. I promise not to post any you don't like."

"Let me see," Iris said, leaning over the table.

Wade couldn't help checking her out in those tight jeans.

"Nice view?" Dena said, smirking at him.

The other girls turned to look at him, and he directed his gaze out the cabin window. "It's a beautiful one."

Iris was back at his side. "I have to go soon."

"What are you, Cinderella?"

"It's not midnight," she said.

"I meant…" He ran his fingers through his hair. The wind had tangled it, and the salty air had curled the ends. "Are you going to turn into a pumpkin if you're not back exactly in two hours?"

"Cinderella doesn't turn into a pumpkin," she said. "It's an actual one that returns to its original state."

"Listen to you being all scientific-sounding," he teased. "I'm so proud."

She elbowed his side. "You're hilarious."

"Oh my God," Violet said, tapping the screen of Carys's phone repeatedly. "Oh my God. Why do you have this photo? How did you get it?"

"What photo?" Dena leaned closer, trying to see over Violet's hands.

Carys glanced over Violet's shoulder at the screen. "*Crap*. I thought I deleted that."

Violet held up the phone, showing the photograph. "This one."

It was the photograph of her and Dena making out in their bras.

"I...I..." Carys looked around at all of them, her eyes pleading for help.

Wade was tired of keeping Carys's secret. He stepped away from Iris. "It's time you two tell her the truth."

"The truth?" Violet asked.

Chapter Thirteen

IRIS

Watching Violet between Dena and Carys, looking confused, tugged at Iris's heart. She wanted to protect Violet from what she was about to hear. What Dena had done wasn't really so bad when she thought about it. An honest mistake. Iris couldn't count how many times she accidentally sent a text to the wrong person.

"I meant to send it to you," Dena was saying. "Instead I sent it to Carys."

"I didn't know it was in my messages," Carys said. "And I didn't know that Marsha would see it come through and go in my phone and send it to herself. I know. I was stupid not to have my screen lock set."

Violet pushed on Dena. "Let me out."

"We didn't mean for it to happen," Dena said, cupping Violet's hands in hers as if she wanted to pray over them or something.

"You took advantage of me while I was drunk." Violet

pushed harder, and Dena slid out of the booth, almost falling over as Violet shoved her so she could get out. "How could you take a selfie of us? I was so out of it." She stomped up the steps.

"I should go with her." Iris gave Wade a quick look. "I'll call you later."

"Do you want me to go with you?" he asked.

"No. I think we need to be alone." She squeezed his hand and scrambled up after Violet.

Violet stormed down the dock.

Iris sprinted to catch up. "Hold on!" she yelled, breathless. "Violet!"

Finally reaching Violet, Iris held her side and kept pace with her. "Don't you want to hear Dena out? So you were drunk. And she was drunk. People do stupid things when they're drunk. Like sending a photo meant for your girlfriend to the wrong number."

"I would never have taken that picture if I wasn't wasted." She frantically searched for her keys at the bottom of her purse. "Dammit. Where are they?"

"Here, let me look." Iris held out her hand. "And I should probably drive."

Violet heaved a sigh before handing her purse over to Iris. "I thought she was the one. Like, we could make a life together. Go off to college. Make a family one day."

Iris gave her a tight hug and held her for many beats before letting go. "You do realize you're only seventeen, right?" She pushed the button on the remote to unlock the doors to Violet's Prius. "What happened to only planning six months in advance? Remember that rule? I believe it's the one you and your shrink came up with."

"Don't call her that. It's rude." Violet opened the door and fell onto the seat. Iris rounded the back of the car and got into the driver's seat. "I'm such a mess." Violet sobbed into her hands. "And Carys. Really? I don't believe Marsha just happened to spot Carys's phone light up right when it received that message. And how could she open, save, and send that pic to her own phone without anyone noticing her do it?" She rubbed away the tears with her fingertips.

"She didn't have to do all that," Iris said. "Only had to forward it. There has to be a message record of it."

Violet gave her a look. "Don't act so smart."

"I have to act. Have you seen my grades?"

"Not funny." She sniffled, holding back a smile.

"I thought it was very funny." Iris brushed the hair away from Violet's tear-drenched face. "I don't know. Do you really think Carys and Dena would intentionally hurt you?"

Next to Wade, Carys was their oldest friend since moving to Ocean City. And Dena loved Violet.

"No. This sucks." She leaned over and rested her forehead on the dashboard. "My heart is breaking. I can't breathe."

It's my fault. I should've fought Crina harder. She had to pull it together. Violet needed her. Her sister's ability to handle this situation concerned Iris. She picked up her phone and dialed her dad's number.

Violet straightened. "What are you doing?"

"Calling Dad."

"No you're not." She went to open the door, and Iris pushed the button to lock it, holding it down so she couldn't get it open.

"I'm concerned."

Violet turned to face her. "I'm not that girl anymore. I can handle this. Promise."

She could hear her dad answer. "Hi, Iris. What's up?"

She looked at Violet.

Violet gave her that pleading look that Iris could never resist.

Iris put the phone to her ear. "Sorry, Dad. I accidentally

dialed you."

"Okay," he said. "How many times have I told you to lock your screen?"

"A million?"

He laughed. "I'll see you at the house later?"

"Yep. See you later." She pushed the hang-up button.

"Thank you," Violet said.

Was she making a mistake? A sinking feeling settled in Iris's gut. "I'll never forgive myself if you do something like you did before," she said.

Violet turned in her seat and looked pointedly at Iris. "Trust me. That girl was weak. This one isn't. I won't kill myself."

Iris nodded. "Okay. I'll trust you. I hope you know that if you ever"—her voice cracked and tears stung her eyes—"I couldn't recover from it. I just couldn't."

"I'm sorry I put everyone through that." Now she was crying again.

"Dena really loves you, Violet. I wish you could forgive her. Besides, she didn't force you to drink."

Violet wiped the tears from her cheeks with her sleeve. "I'm not sure what role Carys played in all this, though."

"I'm not sure, either. But maybe you should give her a chance to explain."

Violet's phone chimed and she glanced at the screen. "It's Dena."

"Answer it."

She tapped the screen. "Hey." She was quiet as she listened to whatever Dena was saying on the other end. "I know. I know. Yeah. I do forgive you. Okay. I'm going home with Iris. I'll see you later, then. Good. I love you, too."

You lose, Crina.

Violet pressed the screen of her phone and placed it on her lap.

Iris chuckled. "That has to be the easiest and fastest makeup I've ever witnessed."

"I guess so." Violet frowned and stared out the windshield. "What should I do about Carys?"

A sharp pain hit her right temple and she moaned, grabbing the side of her head.

"What's the matter?" Violet leaned over and patted Iris's back.

"No, no, no. Go away!"

I see events have transpired while I was gone. You've ruined my plan.

"What is it, Iris?"

"There's a voice in my head. Get her out!" She screamed at another intense stab of pain. Blood trickled from her nose and dropped onto her lap. A bright light flashed across her closed eyelids before darkness strangled the light out and Iris fell back, unable to move until everything vanished—the pain, the light, her awareness.

Hail slapped Crina, pelting her face. She tightened the scarf around her head and held her daughter closer to her chest. Her knuckles stung from pounding on the warped wooden door. Della opened the door, a look of surprise hitting her face. She opened the door wider, snatched up Crina's arm, and towed her inside.

"What are you doing out in this downpour? You will catch the fever."

Rain dripped from the hem of Crina's skirt onto the birch floor. "My love marries that woman tomorrow. I must go to him. Stop him. We could still flee to America. Start a new life."

A cross between sympathy and disappointment shadowed Della's face. "You married Tomas. Go home to your husband.

He loves Oana, and he is good to you."

"No." Crina shook her head. "Please understand. I must try one last time to talk to him. He has to know that Oana is his daughter." She reached the baby out to Della. "Take care of her for me."

Della took Oana into her arms. "When will you return —?"

Crina slipped out the door without another word, the rain surrounding her like a watery curtain.

A faint beeping sounded somewhere in the room. Iris opened her eyes. She wasn't in her home. A sterile smell hinted in the air, and there were ceiling tiles above her.

"You're awake," her dad said, leaning over her. His graying dark hair was messy. Like he'd been there awhile. "How do you feel?"

"Fine." Iris turned her head. "I'm in a hospital?"

"Yes. You fainted in Violet's car," he said. "Do you remember?"

"Yeah. Am I sick?" Her voice sounded scratchy.

He patted her hand before picking up a plastic pitcher on a tray beside the bed and pouring some water into a cup. "You're fine. They can't find anything wrong with you. The scans came back negative. The doctor says it must've been stress." He opened a straw and placed it in the cup.

"Scans? How long have I been out?"

"About eight hours. Here, drink."

Iris lifted her head slightly and took a sip. "Can I go home?"

"I believe so. Once they clear you." He put down the cup. "I'll check. You going to be okay by yourself for a minute?"

She nodded and watched him until he disappeared from her view.

I must say, I don't know my own strength. Crina's voice sounded younger.

"Go away," Iris hissed.

Now, now, is that any way to treat a guest? Do not ever interrupt my game again.

"You sound different. More like my age."

I am stronger and have more control of my voice.

"Why are you showing me your past life?"

What did you see?

"You didn't show me? Your memories are leaking into my thoughts." Iris scooted up the pillows. She grabbed the cup of water on the tray beside her and took a long sip.

What did you see?

"Nothing, really. Just some guy you loved." In the hopes of finding out something she could use from Crina's past, Iris decided not to give details of what she had seen. Iris had gotten good at keeping thoughts from Crina by focusing on something else.

A knock came from the door, followed by footsteps across the floor.

"Hey," Violet said, sitting on the chair beside the bed. "You really gave us a scare."

"Sorry. I haven't been eating or sleeping well."

"Wade was just here. He had to go take his dad somewhere." Violet studied Iris's face for several seconds before speaking again. "You mentioned a voice in your head before you fainted. What did you mean by that?"

Iris decided it was time to tell Violet everything. If she wanted to get rid of Crina, she was going to need all the help she could get. There was no telling what the crazy old spirit could make her do next. Would telling Violet put her in danger? Maybe she shouldn't tell her.

No. NO. You have to tell her, Iris scolded herself. *If she knows, she won't touch those tarot cards, and Crina can't do anything to Violet without them.*

Silly girl, you believe you can undermine me. I am too strong to beat now. She laughed and it was such an evil laugh that it chilled Iris to her core. Dread weighed on her. Crina's next move frightened Iris, but she needed help.

Iris turned her head toward Violet. "I know what I'm about to tell you might sound insane. Might make you think I'm crazy. But—"

I had hoped we could work together, Iris. But seeing that you refuse to cooperate, I shall take over from here.

Violet scooted forward on the seat and grabbed Iris's hand. "Are you okay? I won't think you're crazy. You can tell me anything. I hope you know that."

"I—" Crina-as-Iris cleared the lump of emotion from her throat. "I crave Grandmother's chocolate cake."

"You crave? Grandmother?" Violet furrowed her brows at her. "Okay, what's wrong with you? Stop teasing."

"I should sleep," Crina-as-Iris said. "I am exhausted."

"Yeah, you should definitely take a nap," Violet said. "I'll wake you as soon as we know when you can go home."

Crina closed her eyes. *That did not go so well, did it?*

Please leave me alone, Iris pleaded. *Why are you doing this?*

I thirst for revenge. I live for it. For hundreds of years I have fed on it. I cannot live without its sustenance. As a flower needs the soil, as a fish needs a stream, and as a lion needs a gazelle, I must have revenge. I grow from the depths of its manure. I thrive on it.

You're sick. Iris wanted to cry, wanted to scream, but she had no control over her body. Crina had taken over.

Crina searched Iris's mind, playing images of how she dressed and acted.

That can't be good.

Chapter Fourteen

WADE

Wade leaned against Iris's locker. Since they'd become friends again, they had an unspoken understanding that they'd meet there between classes. He checked the time on his phone and decided to give up, trotting off for his class. It was the third passing period that Iris had ditched him.

Where is she? Hope she's not sick. Iris hadn't looked well lately. She had said it was due to lack of sleep, but he worried it was something more.

He made it to his next class right before the final bell rang.

"Hey," he said to Dena as he slid into his desk.

She tugged her history book out of her backpack. "That was close."

"I was waiting for Iris." Wade unzipped his messenger bag. "She wasn't there again."

"That's strange," Dena said. "She was in her next class when I walked by. Early, even. Sitting straight and proper like she had a board—"

"Okay, class, we have a quiz today, so books away," their teacher, Mr. Shoppe, said.

In her next class? She blew him off. She was sick, all right. Sick of him.

Groans rumbled across the classroom. Wade dropped his book to the floor and pushed it with his foot up against his bag. He rubbed his neck waiting for the copies of the quiz to come down the row. What was going on with Iris? It wasn't like her to blow him off. He could hardly concentrate on the test. Maybe she was giving up on him.

Dena kept glancing his way.

What? he mouthed.

She pointed to the test.

I know. I know, he mouthed again.

He barely finished before time was up. Hoping he had the answers right, he passed his test forward. The bell rang and he practically jumped out of his seat.

"Wade, hold up," Dena said from behind him, but he ignored her.

If Iris was blowing him off, he wanted to hear it from her.

Threading through the packed hallways, he made his way to Iris's locker. She wasn't there again. The hall was loud with excited voices, athletic shoes squeaking across the over-waxed floors and lockers banging shut.

Dena stopped beside him. "Why didn't you wait for me?"

"I can't believe I fell for it again." Wade slammed his open hand against her locker.

"Whoa, calm down, man." Dena glanced around the hall. "You want to get a slip?"

"I don't care."

Just when he was going to slam the locker again, there she was gliding down the hallway as if she hadn't a care in the world. Maybe it was the way she walked or her resting bitch face, but there was something strange about her. He couldn't pinpoint it.

Dena crossed her arms. "Who pissed her off?"

Iris reached them, and her lips pulled into a slow smile. "Hey." When he hadn't responded, she gave him a curious look. "What's wrong with you?"

"What's wrong with me?" he repeated, taking a step back so he could inspect her better. "Where have you been? I've been right here between every class waiting for you."

"Oh, right. We meet between classes."

The confused look on her face made his anger turn to concern. "Did you hit your head when you fainted?"

She shrugged a shoulder. "I just feel a little off since the incident."

"I think you need to eat something," he said. "Come on."

"What did you pack today?" Dena asked, following alongside them.

"Nothing," Wade said. "I stayed up late last night doing homework. You'll have to fend for yourself in the cafeteria line."

Dena's shoulders slumped. "You're killing me. I had high hopes for another one of your gourmet lunches."

Iris was silent during the lunch break. Her eyes switched from Dena, to Violet, to him, not bothering to participate in the conversation. Something serious was going on with her. By the looks Violet was giving him, she was concerned, too.

Wade walked Iris to class after lunch. "How about I pick you up later and we go hang out on the boat."

"That would be fun," she said, leaning closer to him. "What are we going to do?"

"I was thinking I'd grab a pizza," he said. "Bring my laptop. The marina has wifi, so I thought we could watch a movie. You know, get some alone time."

"I like that idea." She gave him a bright smile, but there was something mischievous in her eyes. "Pick me up at my house at six?"

Even her voice sounded different. Wade forced a smile. "Sounds good."

She spun around to go.

"Hey." Wade caught her hand. "I'll walk you to class."

She gripped his hand. "That would be nice."

Nice? She definitely hit her head hard.

When she didn't let go, he laced her fingers with his and walked hand in hand down the hall.

The boat swayed, lightly bumping against the slip. Wade closed the pizza box and piled the used plates and napkins on top of it. Iris popped the last of the crust in her mouth, then chased it down with her Dr Pepper.

"This pizza and drink are delicious." Iris took another swig from her can. "I never tasted something this divine before."

"What's wrong with you?" He crinkled his eyebrows. "You live on Dr Pepper. And why are you talking funny?"

"How so?"

"Like that," he said. "You're in a play again, aren't you?" It was annoying when she'd practice on him. He didn't wait for her response. Instead, he got out of the booth and picked up his laptop. "Let's get comfortable and watch a movie." He led the way to the loft bed in the forward part of the boat.

She slipped off her shoes before hoisting herself up onto the mattress. He followed her in, placing the laptop on the built-in shelf.

"You want a comedy or drama?"

"I like horror flicks," she said.

Flicks? Wade shook his head. "No you don't. Remember the last one we watched? Scared you out of your mind. How about something light?"

"It doesn't matter." She stretched out on the bed. "We won't be watching much of it, anyway."

He clicked on the movie-streaming site and scrolled through the movies. She was definitely seducing him. It concerned him. Which was stupid. What hot-blooded male would resist her? Damn his mom for instilling morals in him. Until he was sure about them, that they could move past the trust issue, it was hands off. If things didn't work out for them, he didn't want her having any regrets.

He clicked on a comedy and scooted over to her, propping up against the pillows.

She laid her head on his chest and nuzzled against his side. He was hyperaware of her hand on his chest and her foot rubbing up and down his leg.

"What are you doing?"

"Getting comfortable," she said.

Concentrate on the movie, Wade.

Her hand twitched slightly, moving down a little, her pinkie just above his belt.

He drew in a calming breath. *Is she doing this on purpose?*

She arched her back, causing her breasts to push against his side and something of his to push against his pants.

"This is nice." Her voice was breathy and tickled his senses.

"It's great," he said, trying to act unaffected.

He wanted her badly, but an inner voice kept nagging at him. *How could you trust her?*

She propped up on one of her elbows so she could look into his eyes. "Why are you resisting all my plays?"

"You're making plays?" He so wished his voice hadn't shuddered over "plays."

With a quick laugh, she crawled on top of him and pressed her lips to his. His hands slid over her back and he pulled her closer to him, deepening the kiss. Her lips parted with a moan and she slipped her tongue in his mouth. She tasted like Dr Pepper.

She straddled him, grasping his shirt. He helped her lift it over his head. She tossed the shirt aside and ran her hands across his chest, sending tingles over his skin. Her lips found his again and she lightly bit his lower lip before kissing his neck and continuing to his chest.

When her hands went to his belt and fingers fumbled with the buckle, Wade snapped out of it.

"Whoa, whoa, whoa, wait." He sat up and scooted away from her. "What are we doing here?"

"I want you," she said through panted breath. "Don't you want me?"

It wasn't about if he wanted her. Because he did. Bad. It would be a dickhead move to refuse what she was offering. But something wasn't right.

She reached out for him. "Come on. I'm ready. I want you."

It was clear to him that he would one day regret this decision. "A guy has to plan for this."

She brushed the hair from her face. "How so?"

"You know."

"No I don't." God. Her skin glistening with perspiration was so hot.

"I don't have a condom."

"What's that?"

He was beginning to think an alien had taken over her body. "A condom. To keep you from getting pregnant and to prevent diseases."

"I don't have a disease." Her shirt was unbuttoned at the top, exposing her bra and part of her stomach. She reached for him again. "We don't need one."

Wade grabbed his shirt and put it on. "It's getting late. I should bring you home before your dad worries."

"You're really something," she snapped, fumbling to button her shirt with shaky hands. "If you don't want me, I'll find someone who does."

"Hey, stop it." He pulled her into his arms. "What's going on with you? Of course I want you. I didn't mean to make you feel rejected. I just think ever since what happened the other day, you're not yourself." He lifted her chin with his finger and looked pointedly into her eyes. "I care about you." He kissed her.

Her eyes popped open and she pushed back from him. "Wade, I do need your help," she said quickly and with great force. "I'm not myself. Talk to Dais—"

Her face scrunched up and she groaned, grabbing her head.

"Iris?" Whatever was happening to her was scaring the shit out of him. "Are you hurt?"

She released her head and smiled up at him. "I just keep getting headaches. I'm fine. The doctor says it's stress. You probably should get me home."

"Okay." He had a sinking feeling something was extremely wrong with her.

Violet would know what to do.

They straightened their clothes before leaving. Wade threw the empty pizza box and used paper goods into the trash can at the end of the docks. Iris on the back of his bike felt different, barely holding on and sitting away from him. Usually, she leaned into him and clenched him tight.

When they arrived at her house, she didn't wait for him to walk her to the door. Instead, she darted up the steps and yelled over her shoulder, "Good evening!"

Good evening? She sounded like her gram.

Before he took off, a thought struck him. After she got a headache, he thought she was going to mention her sister. She said to *talk to Daisy.*

Chapter Fifteen

IRIS/CRINA

Crina slammed Iris's bedroom door. "Unbelievable. Finally free to do whatever I want and you have to be virtuous."

You were going to have sex with him. Iris fumed. *Give me back my body.*

"Poor Iris. Why do you think I'm taking control?" Crina unbuttoned her shirt and slipped it off. "Haven't you wondered? With each cursed fate I give, the closer I get to ridding myself of you forever." She removed her bra, running her hands across her flat stomach. "I do like this body. So pretty you are. So young. Healthy. And impeccably clean."

Don't touch me.

"It's not *me*. It's *us*."

You're evil and old.

"You hurt my feelings, Iris. I was your age when I died. Already a mother, I was."

My age?

"Yes." Crina inspected their shared body in the mirror.

"The longer I have control, the sooner you will turn into the curse. And once you do, I know how to extract you from this body and put you into the cards. I will then destroy them, thus you will be dead. And I will live on."

You're a monster.

"Perhaps." She searched the drawers. "I once was a girl like you. In love. But he betrayed me." She stopped at the drawer that held Iris's pajamas and held up a tank top. "This is horrible. Don't you have something more feminine to wear for bed?"

Iris wasn't going to answer her. They may have traded places, but Iris wasn't weak. Sure, Crina had taken control. But that meant Iris could, too. She would mess up Crina as much as possible. Hopefully someone would notice.

Daisy. I have to get to her. Hopefully Miri found out a way to get rid of Crina.

Dressed in Iris's favorite pajama bottoms and tank top, Crina sat on the bed, shuffling through the tarot cards. "Let's see. Which fate would be best for our next victim? Marsha Simmons. She really is a rotten person. Don't you think? Well, that's silly. Of course you think that."

Part of Iris wanted Marsha to get what she deserved. The bigger part, the one that cared about all living things, even insects, didn't wish her any harm.

"I must say." She spoke, glancing at cards one at a time before tossing them on the bed. "The man who crushed me wasn't as handsome as Wade. Such a wonderful prize I'll have when I've finished exorcising you from this body."

Iris didn't want to listen to Crina and her conquest over Wade. She wished she could just go to sleep and wake up the next morning free of the wretched woman. Or girl. Whatever she was, she was a nightmare.

Crina stopped on a card.

The Devil card? Iris didn't like the looks of that. *What will that do?*

"She's a devil, that one." She rubbed circles on the back of the card until the vines had gone from green to black. "It's fitting. I am not certain what will come of it. She could suffer any number of consequences from fostering all the cardinal sins—pride, greed, lust, envy, gluttony, wrath, and sloth."

Sloth?

"It's being lazy, either spiritually or emotionally." She stood and crossed the room to Iris's backpack on the window seat.

Don't do it. You could save yourself. We could find a way.

Crina threw her head back and laughed. "Silly girl. I don't want saving." Her eyes went to the mirror, and Iris could see herself. She looked like her but different. She couldn't place her finger on it, but she was different. Were her eyes a darker blue? Her face paler? Whatever it was, maybe attitude, it was dark—evil.

"I want to live," Crina said.

I want to live, too. Iris was tired. She had discovered that when that happened, she vanished or slept. She couldn't be sure which one.

The rain hit like cold daggers against Crina's face and arms. Mud grabbed onto her shoes as if trying to keep her from moving forward. In the distance, the castle was ablaze with flickering lights.

It was a painful memory for Crina, and Iris didn't want to be in it.

The old woman is wrong, Crina thought. She had every right to seek revenge. Armand had used her and had thrown her away like a rind of an eaten fruit. Armand could have walked away from his duty, but he chose not to. After Crina told this to the woman, the witch helped her create the curse.

Duty.

Every Van Buren heir would suffer for it.

A sacrifice must be made to seal the curse. The woman had told her. Crina wasn't afraid of what she must do. She was dead already, a corpse walking around without a heart.

The doors to the castle were tall and thick. She had to push her weight against one to open it, the warm light spilling over her. She shivered and headed in the direction of voices—across the foyer and down a wide corridor. The servants were too busy attending the dinner to notice Crina's entrance into the dining hall.

It was a celebration for Armand. He had turned eighteen. With all the riches around him and the fine fabrics of his clothing, he looked different to Crina. Less of a man.

The first person to spot her was Armand's mother. The woman would never be a grandmother to Oana, probably hadn't any knowledge that the baby existed. She pushed out her chair and stood.

"What is this?" Armand's mother glanced at the servants.

The others at the long table, nearly twenty or so men and women, all looked at Crina.

Armand shot up from his seat. "I will take care of the matter." He charged over to her, grabbed her elbow, and led her out of the room. "Why are you here?" he hissed under his breath.

Crina tried to yank her elbow free from his grasp, but his grip tightened, strong fingers digging into her skin.

"You betrayed me," she said loudly, not caring who heard her.

"Hush or I'll—"

"Kill me?" Crina glared at him. "I'm already dead."

"Armand?" A voice so sweet, yet commanding, came from behind them.

Crina looked over her shoulder. Coal-colored eyes met hers. It was as if someone had dressed up a sickly girl from the market—she was pale and beautifully dressed. At the sight of his bride, Crina sagged in Armand's hold. Beaten. Defeated.

Before she realized it, he had her at the front door and shoved her outside. "Now go, and don't ever come here again."

Tears burned Crina's eyes. "You never loved me. What of our daughter? Do you not want to know her?"

"You're married," Armand said. "The daughter belongs to your husband."

"How could you?" she said over a sob.

"Armand? What is happening here?" The girl stopped behind him; her eyes held concern or maybe empathy for Crina, who must have looked like a pauper with her clothes muddied and torn.

Crina almost faltered. The girl was innocent. She had no idea what Armand had done, what he had promised Crina. But the anger on Armand's face and the hatred in his eyes called Crina into action. She pulled the Death card out of the pocket of her skirt.

"You will know my pain, Armand. Your descendants will feel it for years to come." Crina held up the card. "I curse you and yours. All Van Buren firstborn sons will die on their eighteenth birthday." She threw the card. The instant it left her fingertips, it burst into flames and soared across the space between her and Armand. It hit him in the chest, catching his waistcoat on fire.

"Have you lost your mind?" He scrambled out of his jacket, dropped it on the floor, and stamped it out.

She turned and ran, slipping in the mud and falling to her knees.

"Crina!" Armand yelled from behind her.

She got up and sprinted down the road. He was still behind her.

Why is he following me?

It was dark, the moon hidden behind clouds, so dark she

could hardly see in front of her. She passed under a Sleeping Willow, tangling in its branches as she made her way to the river.

"Crina!" Armand called. He couldn't see anything, either.

She tied the hem of her skirt to its waistband, creating a sort of pouch. Gathering rocks, she dropped them into the pouch until it was so heavy she struggled to walk into the water. The river was freezing. With each step in, she sank lower into its depths.

The curse requires a sacrifice. A death. She recalled the old woman's words. *It must be a great sacrifice. The baby would do.* But Crina couldn't kill her baby. The little thing was innocent. Tomas loved her dearly. He was a good man. Crina hadn't deserved him.

I will be the sacrifice.

The water lapped against her chin and she heard him again. "Crina! Please. I am sorry. I truly loved...*love* you. I had no choice... Where are you?"

No choice? You had more than one, Armand. And you chose wealth over love.

Murky water filled her ears and nose and stung her eyes.

Oana's face flickered across her mind—the baby's chubby hand wrapped around Crina's finger as she fed.

Crina panicked. She held her breath and tried to swim, pulling her arms through the water, but the rocks weighed her down and she couldn't move. Darkness closed around her and she inhaled water; her struggle stopped, arms floating lifeless in front of her.

The kitchen smelled like fried bread and fresh oranges. The amount of syrup Crina poured on her pancakes made Iris's teeth hurt. The bottle farted as she squeezed out the last bit. A look passed between Dad and Daisy. Iris only put fresh fruit or peanut butter on her stacks. She hoped Daisy would get suspicious about all the butter and syrup Crina was using.

Daisy smirked at Dad and then went back to cutting her pancakes with her fork.

Come on, Daisy— Iris stopped her thought, fearing Crina would find out what Iris was up to. Daisy had to see that Crina had gained more control over Iris. She needed Daisy to hurry up and find a way to get the spirit bitch out of her.

Iris tried to figure out a way to trip Crina up—how to take back control. Crina was able to push through. Iris had to figure out how to do it.

"So, Iris," Daisy said, stabbing pieces of pancakes to make a tower on her fork. "You must be running out of drops by now; we should get more. I can go with you."

"No, that's okay," Crina said and shoveled a mouthful of dripping cakes into her mouth.

Iris was horrified. If Crina kept eating like that, they'd gain some pounds. *You know that's bad for us, right? I'm mean…don't get me wrong, I splurge at times. But not every day. It'll catch up to us.*

It's my body now. I'll do as I wish with it, Crina snapped.

Iris couldn't see what her dad and Daisy were doing with Crina's head down.

"Are you sure?" Daisy asked. "You could drop me off and I can run in while you wait. Like we did before."

Crina looked up. "I'm not taking them anymore. Trying to eat better, so I won't need them."

A look crossed over Daisy's face, one that was a mix between suspicious and confused.

Look away, Daisy. Don't let her notice you're scrutinizing her.

As if Daisy heard Iris, she went back to stabbing pancakes. "Suit yourself. It's your body."

Crina was amused. *She doesn't know how right she is. It is my body now.*

Iris stayed silent. Her heart, or whatever it was that made her feel in this existence, hurt. She was there with her family, but she wasn't there. Couldn't talk to them. Tell them her feelings. Couldn't feel anything physical, really, but her emotions were all over the place.

When Dad got up to get more coffee at the same time Violet came down the back stairs, Crina was distracted, her eyes going from Dad to Violet. From the corner of her eye, Iris caught a quick glimpse of Daisy as she dropped something into Crina's orange juice.

It had to be Miri's concoction.

Iris waited for Crina to drink it.

And she waited.

"Wow, a full breakfast," Violet said, shuffling into the kitchen. "It's a weekday. What's the occasion?

"Dad didn't stay in his hotel last night. He slept over." Daisy tapped her fork on the table.

Whenever he came to town, Mom would offer him the guest room. But he'd refuse, even when Mom was gone, because his wife would throw a fit.

Guess he's rebelling.

Dad frowned at her fork hitting the wood. "Do you mind?"

She stopped.

Violet sat down with a plate and a glass of juice. She took a sip. "Oh gosh, this is delicious, Dad. I love freshly squeezed juice."

"Thanks," he said. "I'm glad someone appreciates my efforts."

"I appreciate it." Daisy lifted her glass and drank down the juice. She had jumped at the opportunity, and Iris wanted to scream, *Thatta girl!* But of course, she couldn't.

Crina didn't want to look bad in Dad's eyes, so she picked

up her glass and took a long sip. "Oh, this is delicious."

Iris waited for the drops to do their thing. With a full stomach, she wasn't sure they'd have any effect on Crina.

Dad stood, lifted his plate and coffee cup, and took them to the sink. "Okay, Violet, we have to go."

"Ready." Violet grabbed two pancakes and picked up her backpack by the door. "See you at school, Iris."

"Where are you going?" Crina asked.

"Remember, my therapist is every Friday." Violet yanked open the back door. "You have to take Daisy to school."

"Oh, that's right." Crina glanced over at Daisy. "What time do we need to leave?"

"We have about fifteen minutes," Daisy said.

Dad followed Violet out the door.

Daisy got up and grabbed her dishes. "Guess we should clean up."

"Do you know how to drive?" Crina asked, bringing hers to the sink.

"Are you serious?" Daisy glanced over her shoulder.

Crina swayed a little and grabbed onto the side of the counter.

Iris pushed her way forward, concentrating hard to take control of her body.

"Ow," Crina whined and rubbed the side of her head. She stumbled to the table and dropped down on a chair.

Daisy went over to her and placed her hand on Crina's back. "Iris, are you getting a sugar rush or what?"

Iris lifted her head. "That bitch has a sweet tooth, doesn't she?"

"Is it *you* you?" Daisy said.

"Yes." Iris stood. "We have to hurry. I'm not sure how much time we have until she takes over again."

"How did she take over?" Daisy asked.

"I don't know. She just grew stronger than me," Iris said.

"Now listen carefully. I have to get to Wade and tell him what's happening. Find Violet. Her therapist's office isn't too far from here. You know where it is?"

"Yes. I've been there before."

"Good," Iris continued. "Tell her about the curse. About Crina. I need help. Don't text it. Tell her in person. Has Miri found anything from the hatbox that could help me?"

"No," Daisy said. "I'm scared for you."

Iris placed her open palm on Daisy's cheek. "I know. Me, too. You've done great so far. We need a fate changer. Did you get ahold of Aster?"

"No, she wasn't responding to her texts or answering my calls. I'll keep trying."

"Okay. See if you can stay at Amber's house again tonight." What would happen if they couldn't reach Aster in time? Iris swallowed back the emotions building in her throat. She had to be strong for her sisters.

Daisy hugged Iris. "Please be careful."

"I will." She squeezed her back. "Do you have any of Miri's drops left?"

"Yes."

"Put it in everything you know Crina will eat or drink. Like the syrup. Her water bottle. Anything."

They released each other.

"We're going to be okay," Iris said, faking the most reassuring smile she could manage. "One more thing, never take a tarot card from me. It's how she curses people."

"Got it." Daisy lifted up her bag.

"Good. Let's go." Iris grabbed her keys off the counter and her backpack from the bench by the back door. She held the door open for Daisy to go through, then she shut and locked it. As Iris pulled the Bug out of the driveway, she prayed Crina would stay put long enough for her to explain things to Wade.

Chapter Sixteen

WADE

The usual suspects crowded around Josh, listening to his dumb jokes and laughing at the appropriate times. All of them hoping to earn favor from the King of Idiots. Marsha glimpsed Wade as he passed. She flashed him a smile, eyes roaming up and down his body. Wade could feel her stare on his back as he continued down the hall and until he turned the corner.

He adjusted his messenger bag and entered his combination into his lock.

Marsha surprised him when she came up and leaned against the locker beside his. "This biker thing really is working well for you. But you and I know you're far from a bad boy. Wade Diaz, savior of the nobodies and hottest guy at school. You're such a contradiction."

"What do you want?" He searched through his books.

"Is that any way to treat an old flame?"

"One kiss in ninth grade doesn't constitute 'old flame' status."

She straightened and placed her hand on his biceps. "You've been working out."

"Yeah, here and there." He pulled out the book he needed, breaking her grip on his arm, and slipped it into his bag. "So you going to tell me what you want?"

"I wanted to invite you to my Halloween party tomorrow night. You know it's going to be better than the Layne sisters' disaster will be."

"You must fear the competition to ask me to go to yours." Wade slammed his locker shut. "What happened to you? Huh? You and Iris were best friends in eighth grade. She became more popular than you did. Didn't she? That's why you just had to knock her down. Well, you got what you wanted. Why don't you leave us peons alone?"

Marsha frowned and took a step closer to him. "Oh, you don't get it, do you? It was never about how popular she was or that she had Josh. It was always about you. Even after I told her about my feelings, she left Josh and hooked up with you. Friends don't do that to friends." She laughed, a sarcastic one, and her eyes teared a little. "But I guess I'm the bitch, right? Because your precious Iris could do no wrong. Or could she? Don't forget how she suddenly dumped you to get back with Josh." She walked away, discreetly wiping her eyes.

Iris weaved around groups of students, sprint-walking over to Wade. "Hey, we need to talk fast," she said, grabbing his elbow and leading him to the exit. Just outside the doors, she turned to him. "Okay, this is going to sound crazy. Like batshit crazy." She took a breath.

Wade suddenly felt uneasy. She was a mess, shifting her weight anxiously from foot to foot, gripping the handles of her backpack tightly.

"Oh god, I don't know where to start." She took another breath and released it slowly. "I had it all planned out and now I just don't know."

He dropped his hands on her shoulders. "Calm down. Just tell me."

"You're going to think I'm insane." Her eyes went to a guy and girl passing them and going through the exit doors.

"Start at the beginning," he said, removing his hands.

"Okay, so Aster went to a tarot card reading last year. And—" She squinted her eyes tight before continuing. "And she had a reading." She rubbed her temples.

"Are you getting another headache?"

She nodded and glanced up, her eyes half opened. "Where was I?"

"Aster and tarot cards," he reminded her.

"I'm out of time. I'm not myself." She flinched and bent over. "Talk to Daisy."

"Hey." He wrapped his arm around her back, supporting her. What was going on with her? He couldn't believe the doctors hadn't found anything wrong. "Maybe we should go to the nurse's office."

She straightened. "I'm fine. Just ate too many pancakes this morning."

Fine? He doubted it. She was anything but fine.

"What do you want me to talk to Daisy about?" he asked, not sure if she was okay or just faking it.

"I said that?" She smoothed down her shirt.

"Yeah, and something about Aster and tarot cards?"

"Oh, I was just wondering if you thought it would be a good idea to have Daisy be a tarot card reader at the party." She adjusted the backpack on her shoulder. "Astor had dressed up as one before. We have all the stuff. Just thought it would be cool to add one, since we have that drinking game with the cards."

"Sure, but why do I have to talk to her? Why don't you just ask her?"

"Because she won't do it for me, but she will for you." She

touched his cheek. "No one can resist you."

He chuckled. "You've resisted me before."

"I'm claiming temporary insanity on that one."

Wade laughed and snatched up her hand. "I'd say you were insane. Come on, we'd better get to class."

As they walked through the doors, Iris lightly slapped his chest. "That isn't funny. I'm not insane."

Marsha passed, glaring at them.

There he was again holding her hand and walking her to class. It felt natural to him. He could do this. It was time to take the next step. Wade was tired of fighting his feelings. He wanted her badly, to the point it hurt.

"Just a minute," Iris said and walked after Marsha. She called her name and Marsha turned around.

Wade trailed her.

Marsha crossed her arms and frowned at Iris. "What do you want?"

"Nice outfit," she said, inspecting Marsha's attire. "How do you stay so thin?"

Marsha gave a look at Wade before answering, "Discipline."

"Must be. Anyway, I wanted to invite you to our party." Iris removed a tarot card from the outside pocket of her backpack and handed it to Marsha.

Marsha gave the card a curious look. "No thank you."

"Just take it," Iris urged, stretching out the card. "You never know, you may just want to stop by."

Marsha rolled her eyes. "If it will get you to leave me alone—" She grabbed the card. "Ouch. Use a Bounce sheet or something next time. You shocked me." She strutted off in her high heels as if she was on a Paris runway.

Iris laced her arm around Wade. "So I read in the newsletter that the drug dogs are inspecting our lockers today."

"I'd better hide my stash, then," Wade joked. "Marsha's having her own party. Why did you invite her to ours? She'll suck the fun out of it."

"It was a peace offering. You needn't worry. She won't come."

They stopped in front of Iris's classroom. He wondered if they should talk about the other night on the boat. She didn't seem awkward about it. If she really was ready to take their relationship to the next level, he was game. Hell, he was more than game.

As if she was reading his mind, she leaned close to him. "You know, we could ditch and go to my house. No one's home."

Maybe they should. She had declared her love for him. And he knew how he felt about her. It was a natural next step. He'd imagined having sex with her many times. It was on a repeating loop playing in his dreams most nights.

His phone vibrated in his front pocket and he tugged it out. It was a text from Violet.

We need to talk. I'll be back at school soon. Lunch? Behind the baseball bleachers. Don't say anything to Iris. IT'S IMPORTANT. Don't tell her you're meeting me or about this text.

He looked up at Iris. "My dad. He's back home."

"That's great." She seemed disinterested as she watched the kids rushing to class. "So are we ditching?"

"No. I have a test. How about a rain check?" He slipped his phone back into his pocket. "I've got to get to my class. See you later."

She pushed him against the lockers. "You sure?" She reached up and kissed him. Her hand ran along his thigh and heat rose in his pants. Her kiss deepened as her hand traveled around to his butt and she lightly squeezed it.

"Get a room," a guy grunted as he hurried past them into Iris's class.

"We're going to get a PDA write-up."

She pulled away from him. "I just wanted to show you what you'll be missing."

"Oh, I know what I'm missing. Trust me."

"Well, I'll be thinking of you." She sauntered off and followed the guy into her room.

Wade's Doc Martens thudded against the tiled floor as he sprinted down the hallway. He mentally kicked himself. It seemed like forces were in play, keeping Iris and him from going all the way. The frustration was building inside him. Most guys his age were getting it all the time from their girlfriends. Hell, Dena had more action with Violet than he had with Iris.

Violet was pacing behind the bleachers when Wade arrived. He hoped it didn't have anything to do with Dena. After Violet found out that she was the one who took the pic, she had forgiven her. Carys hadn't been as lucky. Violet wasn't sure about Carys's role in Marsha getting ahold of the photograph. Maybe this meeting had something to do with that.

At hearing his boots crunch against the gravel, she glanced at him. Her mascara was smudged under her eyes and red streaks marked her chest. Scratching her chest was a nervous habit she had.

"What's wrong?" he asked.

"I just left Daisy." She started pacing again. "She ditched school and was home when my dad dropped me off to get my car."

"Okay. Do you need me to talk to her?" He was getting dizzy watching her. "You could call your mom or Gram.

They'd know what to do. When do they get back?"

"Mom will be home on Sunday. Gram another week. But they can't help." She stopped and looked over at him. "It's about Iris. I need your help."

"Sure. What's going on?"

She took several steps and gave him a tight hug. "You're going to think I'm crazy, but don't say anything until I'm done."

Everyone's crazy lately or thinks they are, anyway.

Wade was starting to think that he was the only sane one these days. From Dena and the Bra-gate incident to Iris and her sudden sex drive and to all the strange things in between, some lunar phenomenon had to be causing it. Like an asteroid heading for Earth or something.

Chapter Seventeen

Iris/Crina

Crina walked down the hallway, not bothering to look for Wade. The school was buzzing with the latest rumor. She smiled, stopping beside Carys to watch while police officers escorted Marsha outside.

"What's going on?" Crina acted innocent.

Carys uncrossed her arms. "They found Molly in her locker."

Molly? Crina thought. *Did she kill a girl, chop her up, and stuff her in the locker?*

Iris mentally rolled her eyes. *Yeah, she'd do that at school. With everyone around. It's a drug, moron.*

"That's unfortunate," Crina said.

Carys noticed the smugness in her voice. "I'm sure you're worried for her. Karma's a bitch, right?"

"I haven't met her, but if you say so," Crina answered.

Carys laughed. "I hope you never do unless she's nice."

What am I missing? Crina asked Iris.

More than you know. Iris refused to help her anymore, but then wondered if she didn't, would Crina do something bad to her?

"So are we still friends?" Carys asked.

"Of course we are. I couldn't care less what Violet thinks." Crina headed down the hall, and Carys kept up with her.

"Am I still invited to the party tomorrow night?"

Crina spotted Josh by the bathroom doors and stopped. "Yes, and you're coming in the morning to set up, right?"

"I'll definitely be there," Carys said, excitement lacing her words. "I was thinking of bringing this guy from my science class, but we haven't defined our relationship yet."

"What do you mean by that?"

Carys opened her mouth to say something but stopped. Iris mused that she most likely was going to ask if Crina had hit her head. But instead, she said, "I think he'd rather me be a booty call than a girlfriend."

Crina's gaze went to Josh again.

"Pardon me, I have something to do." Crina slipped off her sweater as she crossed the hall to Josh. "Sorry to hear about your girlfriend."

"I bet you are." Josh's eyes lowered to her chest.

Why is he checking out my boobs? Iris seethed.

Because this shirt is giving him an eyeful, Crina answered.

Of what?

Your breast. What did you call me earlier? Oh yeah, moron.

Crina took a few steps forward until she was too close to Josh for Iris's comfort. "I guess you won't be throwing that party after all."

"Guess not," he said.

"I have something for you." She handed him a tarot card, and he flinched when it shocked him.

"What's this for?"

What card is it? What curse are you giving him?

Hush. You're going to mess me up, Crina scolded her.

Crina ran her hand down his arm. "It's how you get into our party. I'd love to see you there."

"What about your boyfriend?"

Yeah. What about Wade?

"We haven't defined our relationship." Crina sounded so sweet, it made Iris want to barf. If she had control of her own body, she probably would have. "A girl can wait only so long," she said. "I miss you."

"You do?" He leaned closer to her.

"And I'm ready."

Josh dropped the card in his hand. They both glanced down at it. It was the Tower card. He bent over and picked it up.

What curse is that? Iris asked.

You are such an annoyance. It could be literal or metaphoric. He could fall off a tower or become withdrawn.

You're sick. How can you do this to people? Hurt people.

I'm a spirit. I care not for mortals. When you stop thinking of me as human, you will understand me better.

"What are you ready for?" Josh asked.

"I don't want to be a virgin forever," she whispered in his ear, a breathy one that made him shudder. She straightened and before she walked off, she said, "Bring condoms."

Iris wanted to scream. *What are you doing?*

"I'll be there," Iris heard him say behind her.

You are not having sex with him. NO way.

Crina laughed. *It amuses me that you think you have a say in what I do.*

If Iris thought her nightmare couldn't get any worse, she was wrong. She stared at the reflection of herself as Crina combed long bleached strands. Her hair! The bitch had bleached her hair.

When did you do that? Iris asked.

"While you were sleeping."

Kill me now.

Crina smiled at the reflection. "Soon."

Why can't I know your thoughts like you can mine?

"You're not evil enough. I've been a cursed spirit for ages." She placed the brush on the dresser. "I can search your memories. Learn how to talk. Well, I'm still working on that one, but it will come to me in time. And the hair is fabulous. It'll look great with my costume."

You think I'm weak, but you should never underestimate love. I won't let you hurt my family. My friends. Wade. Even that jerk Josh.

Crina threw her head back and cackled, her voice raspy and craggy. She covered her mouth with her hand.

Be careful there. Your ugly is showing.

She glared at the mirror as if she could see Iris within her. "Only time will tell."

Crina stepped downstairs. "Now to find your bratty little sister. Exactly why does she want to talk to Wade? What have you two been conspiring about behind my back?"

You leave her alone. She doesn't know anything.

"You're a poor liar." She stepped out on the porch.

Violet, Dena, Carys, and Lauren were busy setting up the haunted house. Two large canopies with long, dark tarps draped over them stretched across the driveway, connecting the garage and apartment to the main house.

Inside the makeshift tent, the cardboard panels with Iris's paintings of a spooky graveyard and creepy laboratory served as the walls. Cutouts of vampires, werewolves, and other scary paranormal creatures held up by stands that Wade had constructed stood around the room. The coffins he'd made surrounded the open area. The canopy and tarps breathed in and out with the breeze coming off the ocean, and the scent of paint and glue washed over her.

Carys and Lauren busied themselves hanging cobwebs while Dena and Violet worked on assembling the blue-light lamps. They all stopped what they were doing when Crina walked up.

"Your hair," Violet said, standing.

Crina brushed her fingers through it. "You like it? I needed a change."

Violet just blinked. She was as stunned as Iris had been when she first saw it.

Lauren smiled brightly, but it was more forced than genuine. "Love it. It fits you."

"Yeah, it'll take some time to get used to," Dena said, "but you rock it."

"Thank you." Crina glanced around. "This is fabulous. I couldn't imagine what it would be like once all the pieces were put together, but it's impressive."

"Your art made it come to life," Lauren said. She was so trying too hard. Iris felt sorry for Lauren. Fitting in was difficult. Everyone wanted to have a posse. Friends who understood you and who had your back whenever the bad times rolled around. Maybe she had learned her lesson. If Iris ever got her life back, she would be more like Violet and show Lauren forgiveness. Welcome her into their group.

"Where's Daisy?" Crina asked.

Leave her alone. Iris pushed and pushed to take over this screwed-up possession thing.

Stop. Crina sounded annoyed. *I'm too strong for you, and you'll succeed only in giving us a headache.*

Violet brushed some hair that had escape her bun away from her face. "Daisy's at a friend's house. Dad is in Baltimore until Sunday night. Remember, no one is allowed in the house.

That way cleanup will be easy tomorrow."

"What if we have to take a piss?" Dena said, draping her arm around Violet.

"I hate that word," Violet said. "There's a bathroom in the apartment for everyone to use."

Wade walked up the driveway carrying two paper trays filled with coffee cups. "I've got fuel." They all crowded around him like pigeons on a dropped piece of bread. He passed out the coffees, handing one to Crina. "Caramel latte for my girl."

She smiled. "Thank you."

"How did your dad like the boat?" Dena asked, slowly sipping her coffee.

"He loved it," Wade said. "Got all emotional. We had a good run. The wind speed was perfect today. "

Crina took a drink from her cup, burning her tongue. "Oh, this is hot but delicious."

"I told them extra caramel for you," Wade said.

Extra caramel? Iris never would ask for that. She'd want to taste the coffee not the added flavor.

Wade snaked around the cutouts and coffins, inspecting the work so far. He kept glancing over his shoulder at Crina, a strange look on his face. Had Crina noticed it? Crina kept sipping her coffee down as she watched Violet.

It is strange having someone who looks exactly like yourself walking around. Did you ever feel that way? Crina slurped some more of her drink through the slit on the top of the coffee cup.

No. Iris noticed Violet sneaking glimpses at Crina, too. *We've been together since birth. It's all we ever knew.*

Crina rocked on her feet and dropped her cup. *Why are you trying to take over? We both would do much better if you'd just let go.*

Iris wasn't doing anything. She had tried but wasn't strong enough. Daisy. Crina must have consumed something with the drops in it.

When Crina was in control, Iris felt like she was bound by ropes and chains, unable to operate her own body. It was as though she was paralyzed and disconnected from everyone. Alone. That was it. She was so alone that the darkness and silence was a razor blade to her heart. A metaphoric one, since her physical body was no longer in her control.

Crina rubbed her head as if she could get rid of the headache consuming them.

Wade hurried over to her and supported her by the elbow. "Hey, do you need to sit down?"

"I'm fine," she snapped and tried to pull away from him, but he wouldn't let go.

When the pain lifted, Iris was back in control. "Wade?"

He looked into her eyes. "Iris, is it you?"

"You know?"

Wade nodded. "Yes. Daisy told us. She's with Miri trying to find a way to get rid of the curse."

Iris fell against him and sobbed. He held her so she wouldn't collapse to the ground. She spotted Violet and the others glancing at them.

Violet set her coffee on a coffin and rushed to them. "Iris?"

"It's her," Wade answered.

As Violet went to hug Iris, Wade let go.

"I was worried you wouldn't believe Daisy."

Violet stepped back, grasping Iris's arms and holding her stare. "You are part of me. Of course I knew it wasn't you. Well, I didn't know you were possessed, just that some crazy shit was going on in your head."

A short laugh escaped Iris. "I'm just so tired, and I don't know how long I'll be here. She's going to kill me off. Take over my body. I-I don't know how to stop her."

"We'll find a way. Everything to drink or eat at the party

is going to have Miri's concoction in it." She wiped the tears from Iris's face with her thumbs. "Keep your emotions in check so she doesn't know. Each time you come back, we'll work on getting rid of her. Miri and Daisy will be at the party. We can beat her. All right?"

Iris nodded. "Okay. Having you guys with me, I feel less alone. Less scared."

Violet released her arms, and Wade immediately held her to his chest, kissing her forehead. "You're not alone."

She glanced up at him. "You're amazing, you know that? And I'm sorry she's been frustrating you. Thank you for resisting her."

"It hasn't been easy." He smiled down at her, then lifted her chin and kissed her so gently that it felt like a whisper on her lips. "I love you, Iris."

"What about what I did? You know—"

Wade put his finger over her lips. "Stop. I know everything. Aster changed our fate." He dropped his hand. "I have to admit, I had a hard time believing it until Daisy showed me."

"Showed you what?"

"Daisy's a fate changer, Iris." Violet said it as if Daisy had a serious illness. "She used FaceTime to show us her changing the fate of one of Miri's clients. Her gift is spotty. It doesn't always work, but she's practicing."

"No." She shook her head. "Daisy can't do it. I don't want Crina anywhere near her. We have to get Aster. She has experience with this stuff."

The concern in Violet's eyes mirrored hers. "We'll do everything we can to get Aster here, but if we can't, we need Daisy."

Iris doubted there was a way to stop Crina. She was spiraling, plunging into a place where there was no hope.

Chapter Eighteen

Wade

The Ocean City boardwalk was quiet as Wade pounded on the door of the small white house with red-trimmed windows. The neon sign with Tarot Card Readings on it was off and the one in the window said it was Closed. He shifted, anxious to find a way to help Iris. The desperation burned like hot coals in his chest. His fist landed on the wood again.

"Come on already," he hissed, heat rushing to his face.

Wade peered through the crack in the heavy drapes covering the large window beside the door. He spotted movement and, shortly after, the door opened.

About time.

A woman somewhere near seventy with tight, dark curls, wearing tan-and-black-striped pants and a Jim Morrison T-shirt, opened the door.

Her eyes traveled down him. "Hot. Cuban. Biker. All the boxes checked. You must be Wade."

"I am. Is Daisy here?"

"I'm Miri. We've been expecting you. Come in." She widened the door to let him pass, then escorted him to a room with several posters of The Doors on the walls. Painted on one of the walls was a multicolored mural of Jim Morrison without his shirt on. He had seen the popular image of the rock star floating around the internet. A quote just below it made Wade feel uneasy thinking of Iris. It read, *"Love cannot save you from your own fate."*

When Wade entered the room, Daisy popped up from her seat at a circular table covered in a purple tablecloth. "I'm so glad you're here."

"You look tired," he told her as they gave each other a quick hug.

"I can't sleep. I've been so scared about Iris."

"Me, too, Dais," he said, using his nickname for her. How had she grown so fast? It seemed like yesterday she was ten and building sandcastles with him. There was something special about Daisy. She would never harm anyone. She was always saving spiders and other small creatures before Grams could exterminate them. And Wade would do whatever it took to keep her safe.

Miri sat down on one of the chairs around the table. "Sit. We have much to discuss."

Daisy returned to her seat while Wade settled into one on the other side of her.

"We've searched through all the notes and records in this hatbox," Miri said, tapping a round off-white box with a ribbon securing the top. "And we found the answer. As you know, our problem is that only a fate changer can rid this spirit from Iris."

There was that name again. *Fate changer.* When Violet and Daisy first told him about it, he thought they were insane. After they showed him Daisy change a fate, he started to believe them, but he still had his doubts. He hadn't been fully convinced until Iris came out from behind that spirit. There had been a change in Iris. There was something very wrong with her. But he never thought it was this—this crazy shit.

"I just got off the phone with Aster right before you got here," Daisy said. "The earliest flight she and Reese could get won't arrive until late tonight."

"We'll just have to hope she gets here in time," Wade said. "So what did you need me to do?"

Miri slid a look at Daisy. "I don't think we should *just hope* she arrives before Iris is lost forever. Daisy has agreed to hide nearby the party, waiting in case she's needed."

"Okay, let's do that," Wade said. They had the answer. Iris could be back to normal in no time.

"It's not that simple," Miri said. "I must have Aster's tarot deck. Daisy has to claim them as her own in order to destroy the curse."

Wade stood. "Then I'll go get them for you."

Daisy slumped into her chair. "That's a problem. The deck is in Iris's room, and she's handed out a few cards. We need all the cards. It has to be a complete deck."

"Who did she give them to?" Wade asked.

"I made a list from what Iris told me." Daisy picked up a slip of paper from the table and handed it to Wade. "How can we get them all?"

"It'll be easy to get them from Lauren, Dena, and Carys." He took out his phone and sent a group text to them. "Okay, so the cards from Perry and Marsha might be tough to get. I'll start with Perry. I know him from basketball. He's not that bad a guy. Just hangs with the wrong crowd."

"I'm coming with you," Daisy said, getting to her feet. "It would drive me nuts waiting around here."

"Good idea," Miri said as she stood. "I'll see you both later. I must get into character for the party. I've been hired to read fortunes." She winked. "Text me when you have the cards."

Daisy was quiet on the ride over to Perry's house. Understandable, since it was difficult to speak over the motorcycle's loud engine. That never stopped Iris. She would yell as loudly as it took to be heard or she'd wait for stops when it was quieter.

Perry was shooting baskets in the portable hoop in his driveway when Wade stopped the motorcycle in front of his house.

Daisy slipped off the back of the bike. "I thought he was caught stealing. Shouldn't he be in jail or something?"

Wade took her helmet and put it on the seat. "Must be out on bail."

"What are you doing here?" Perry asked and took a shot. The ball hit the back of the board and fell into the net.

"Good shot," Wade said, walking up the driveway to him. "What's going on?"

Perry rested the ball on his hip. "Other than my entire life's screwed up?"

"Well, stealing was a bad idea," Daisy said.

"I didn't do it," Perry said, dropping the ball. It hit the driveway and rolled into the grass. "My car was there, but it wasn't me. The security camera shows a guy with a black hoodie over his head. You can't see his face. But it was Josh. He borrowed my car that day."

"That sucks," Wade said. "You have a lawyer?"

"Yeah, he doesn't believe me. Neither do my parents." He narrowed his eyes at Wade. "You didn't come by to check on me. What do you want?"

"Iris gave you a tarot card," Wade said.

"We need it back," Daisy finished.

"Why?" Perry asked.

Wade was about to lose his patience. Every minute they wasted was a minute Iris was being tortured by that spirit.

"Just get it. We need it for the party."

Perry flinched at the anger in Wade's voice.

"Sure. Whatever." He headed for the house. "I'll be right back."

When he'd closed the door, Daisy turned to Wade. "You know, Josh came by one day in that car." She pointed at a beat-up white Mustang on the street. "He wanted to get back with Iris. She turned him away. It was Labor Day. I wonder if it was the same day as the robbery."

"That's interesting," Wade said.

Perry returned and handed the card to Wade.

"Thanks, man." Wade turned to leave.

"Where are we going next?" Daisy asked him.

"To see Marsha. Iris gave her a card at school."

Perry picked up his basketball. "You won't find her home. She's in rehab."

"Oh, no," Daisy squeaked. "We need her card."

Perry took out his phone and sent a text to someone. "She has a burner phone. That girl finds a way around restrictions. She keeps it in her bra. The vibration will alert her and she'll say she has to use the restroom or something. Rehab won't help her."

They waited for a response.

Daisy nodded at Perry and mouthed, *Tell him.*

Wade blew out a breath. He didn't want to get involved with matters dealing with the police. Things always went wrong when he had. And it never went well for his mom's campaign, even if he was just a witness. He looked back at Perry. But Perry didn't deserve having something he hadn't done pinned on him.

Perry's phone dinged and he glanced at the message. "It's in her locker."

Wade heaved a sigh. "So when was the game store break-in?"

"Labor Day weekend," Perry said.

A text chimed on Wade's phone. He tugged it out of his pants pocket and walked to his motorcycle. "Go ahead and tell him, Daisy."

She told Perry about Josh going by to see Iris that day. She agreed to talk to Iris about being a witness for him before hurrying to the bike.

"By the way," Perry called and jogged over to them. "The drugs. That was Josh's Molly. He had Marsha stash it in her locker for the party. He can bully anyone into doing things for him. It's time he takes the fall."

"That's not surprising," Wade said. "One day, Josh will get what's coming to him."

"Who sent you the text, Wade?" Daisy said, slipping on her helmet and getting on the seat behind him.

"Iris…um, I mean, Crina." He put on his helmet and started his bike. "She's getting suspicious that I'm not there to help set up things."

"What did you say to her?"

Wade's finger ran across his phone's screen. "I told her my dad needed me. I'm now texting a friend I know to help us get into Marsha's locker."

Daisy and Wade waited outside the back doors of their school. That he might lose Iris tore at his gut. He wanted to fix it. Make her safe. The fact that spirits were real, that there was a place to go after this life, was reassuring and creepy as hell.

Especially when some evil bitch has possessed the girl I love.

It seemed like they'd been waiting forever before his friend, Derick, showed up. "If my dad finds out I took his keys, he'd bust my butt." He jingled the keys.

Wade handed Daisy his helmet. "You wait here. If you see anyone coming, hide. I don't want you getting caught with us."

"Seriously?" Daisy put his helmet next to hers on the

bike's seat. "I'm going with you. I'm too freaked out to be alone."

Wade gave her a firm look. "No. You're not."

"You can't stop me." Daisy crossed her arms.

He could stop her. But maybe she was right. Someone could spot her waiting outside the door and come investigate.

"Okay, but if we get caught, you forced me to take you along. Your sisters will kill me if you get into trouble."

Derick tried another key. "Got it," he said as he unlocked the door and held it open for them.

"Did you bring the bolt cutters?" Wade asked as he passed them.

"They're in the janitor's closet. I'll get them." He let the door slam behind him and shuffled down the hall.

"Way to wake up the dead," Wade said, and Daisy's eyes went wide at that. "What? Don't freak out, it's just a saying."

"It's too close to home." Daisy walked down the row of lockers lining the hall. "Do you know which one is hers?"

Wade trailed her. "It's the one with a heart scratched into the paint. Has J plus M in the middle."

"Here it is," Daisy said, stopping. "Way to deface school property, Marsha."

Derick hobbled up the hallway, the bolt cutters weighing him down on one side.

Wade took the cutters from him. "If we get caught, we'll just say the door was left open."

"We can't do that. My dad will get in trouble for it." Derick glanced in each direction of the hallway. "Just hurry so we don't."

Wade cut the lock off and it fell, clattering against the tiles.

Daisy picked up the lock. "Now who's waking the—" She stopped herself from saying it.

Wade smirked and rattled open the locker door.

"It's empty," Daisy said.

Derick peered inside. "The narcs must have taken her things when they did the search."

"Shit." Wade slapped the locker beside it and seethed.

"Really?" Daisy frowned at him. "Why don't you just break your hand? 'Cause that will help us."

It was a dumb thing to do, but he was frustrated. They needed that card. They couldn't save Iris without it.

A noise came from somewhere in the school. "What's that?" Wade asked.

"Someone's here. We'd better run," Derick said, taking the bolt cutters from Wade. "I'll put these away. Hurry up and I'll be right there." He scuffled off in the direction of the janitor's closet.

Daisy paused as she turned to go. "Wait a minute. There's something stuck in there." She stretched her hand inside and placed her finger on the corner of what looked to be a card sticking up from the locker below. Pressing it against the metal of the locker, she carefully slid it up.

Wade looked over her shoulder. "Careful or you'll lose it."

"Shh…" she hissed. "I'm trying to concentrate. I know, I'll hold it in place while you get it."

He reached in and grabbed it. A red devil with ram horns, bat wings, and talons sat above a naked man and woman. "Well, it's definitely the Devil card."

"What are you two doing?" Derick whisper-hissed, running up to them. "Let's go. It's Mrs. Dunn. She comes in on weekends to grade her students' artwork."

They hurried out the door.

Wade clapped Derick's back. "Thanks, man."

"No problem."

Daisy got on the bike behind him and he drove off. Wade was relieved to have the cards, but he wondered what was next. He wasn't sure how the magic was going to work.

He turned the corner, and the ocean came into view. The moon was barely visible in the late-afternoon sky. He wanted to race to Iris, but he kept to the speed limit, since Daisy was on the back. They'd retrieved all five cards that Crina had given to Marsha, Perry, Lauren, Dena, and Carys. Now, all he had to do was step back and let Miri and Daisy do their magic.

Chapter Nineteen

Iris/Crina

Crina stood in front of the upright mirror in the corner of Iris's room, spinning around to see how she looked. She wore a long green skirt and a lacy corset of the same color. Under her left eye was a swirly inked rune. Her lashes were heavy with winged liner and fake eyelashes. Bloodred lips, ratted platinum hair, and long black press-on nails with sharp points finished the look.

"Tonight, you shall have a fun show. When I've completed dealing fates out to the seven who represent the cardinal sins, you will die, and I will completely take over your body."

I don't understand. What sins? Iris was tired. She'd come in and out of control of her body all day.

"The seven deadly ones, of course—greed, envy, pride, sloth, gluttony, lust, and wrath."

You're not making any sense.

"I have chosen your friends wisely. Not randomly. Lauren has always been envious of your friendships and popularity.

That is why I gave her the Hermit card."

She spun around again. "Don't I look amazing? Anyway, then there was Perry. He never shared anything. Refused to help those less fortunate than himself. He had taken from others before, untrustworthy himself—ridiculing and hurting others. Full of greed, that one. So naturally, I had to give him the Justice card."

Why are you telling me this?

"Because when I was alive, I possessed all the sins. We all do to an extent, but some of us give in to them at the cost of others. My hatred consumed me. I cursed an entire family because of it."

You almost sound like you regret it. Iris wasn't sure what to think. She wanted to know more. There was something to all this. Something she was scared to hear but believed she needed to know. To get her life back. *And the others. They weren't bad, but you gave them cursed tarot cards.*

"Dena," Crina said. "Her pride kept her from telling Violet that she had accidentally sent that photograph to Carys. So the Hanged Man is what she got. He stands for inaction, getting caught."

Crina brushed some white powder on her face. "There. I look paler—like death."

Why Carys?

"Her sin is sloth. She did nothing. Wouldn't tell your sister what truly happened. So it was the reversed High Priestess card. Mistrust."

And Marsha. The Devil card.

"Naturally. She is evil to her bones. That one is gluttonous."

And Josh. The Tower card you gave him, what does that do?

Crina heaved a sigh, and Iris wondered how she could even breathe in that tight corset. "I am tiring of your babble in my head. Josh's sin is lust. He lusts for power, for material things, and for females. He will fall from his tower."

A scary darkness squeezed against Iris. *There's one sin left. Wrath. Whatever the hell you're doing—righting your wrongs? Passing on your bad deeds?—I will stop you.*

"I haven't a conscience. And am not in need of atonement." Crina picked up the tarot deck from the bed, took one, slipped it down the front of her corset, and stuffed the rest between the mattress and box spring. "I must rid our body of the curse so I can grow stronger. You get weaker as I increase my strength. You can't stop me. Once all the sins are dealt and fates played out, I will be free of you."

She spun around one last time, checking herself out before leaving the bedroom and going downstairs. Violet and Dena were deep in conversation when Crina came out the back door. Dena was dressed like a zombie police officer and Violet looked like a corpse bride.

Violet frowned at Crina's outfit. "You were supposed to be a scary witch," she said. "Not a sexy one."

"Not to worry," Crina said. "I will be a nightmare."

Iris noticed the flash of fear in Violet's eyes. She tried to keep that thought from Crina so as not to alarm her. Because why would Violet fear her sister unless she suspected an evil spirit possessed her?

Daisy came out of the makeshift tent dressed as an ancient tarot card reader or an ultra–covered up belly dancer.

No, Daisy! You shouldn't be here. Iris waited for a response from Crina, but none came.

Daisy's skirt jingled as she crossed the driveway. "Would you like your fortune read?" She held a deck in one hand and a few of the cards fanned in the other.

Iris's gut clenched right before Crina barked, "Where did you get those?"

Daisy un-fanned the cards and returned them to the deck in her hand. "No need to get so snappy. We bought several for the game. Want to taste the punch Carys made? You can hardly taste the alcohol in it."

Violet put her fists on her hips and looked sternly at Daisy. "Have you been drinking it?"

"Jeesh, calm down," Daisy said. "I only tasted it. Carys needed to know if there was enough punch in the vodka."

Crina forced a smile. "Lead the way, Daisy. A strong drink is just what I need." She followed Daisy into the tent.

Lauren, dressed like a patient with a fake cut across her throat and a large bloodstain drenching the front of her, was holding a vodka bottle while Carys, wearing bloody scrubs with a stethoscope draped around her neck, fended her off with a spoon. "We don't need any more of that. It's too much already."

"You can hardly taste it," Lauren protested.

"It's vodka," Carys snapped. "It's tasteless."

"I'll be your taster." Crina's heels *click-clack*ed across the concrete drive as she went over to the punch bucket and picked up the ladle. "What's that floating in there?"

"Skulls," Carys answered.

"And fingers," Daisy added. "A real witch's brew. I added a few cockroaches, too."

Crina dropped the ladle and wrinkled her nose at Daisy.

"What? They're plastic." Daisy took a red cup off the stack by the bucket and handed it to Crina. "Did you think I put real ones in it?"

"No." Crina snatched the cup from her. "It just sounded gross."

Wade came around the flap separating them from the main area of the tent. He was dressed like a mad scientist. His hair was a mess with gray paint at the sides. Green gook and blood stained his lab coat. "Hey, Violet said there was punch. I could sure use a cup." He went to Crina and slid his arm around her waist. "You look way too sexy to be an evil witch."

"Iris didn't get the memo," Lauren said. "We were supposed to wear scary costumes, remember?"

"A memo?" Crina looked from Wade to Lauren as she emptied a ladle full of punch into her cup. *What is that?*

Iris wanted to laugh. *You're not learning how to be me very well. And if you get rid of me, you'll lose your point of reference.*

Stay out of my thoughts, Crina fumed.

Wade laughed. "Way to play dumb."

"I'm not dumb." She tipped her cup to her mouth, draining the liquid inside.

"Hey, go easy there," Wade said. "It's a long night. You should pace yourself or you'll get sick." He took the cup from her. "So how does my costume look?"

"You could use some more black around your eyes," Daisy said. "You don't look insane enough."

Wade squeezed Crina's waist. "You want to do me up?"

She gave him a quizzical look. "What?"

"Can I use your eyeliner?"

"Oh, that." She glanced around at the faces staring back at her. Iris could feel a headache coming on, and she was pretty sure Crina was beginning to suspect something.

Trying to keep her thoughts from Crina was making Iris tired. She prayed the drops in the punch would work soon and she could come through. She worried it wouldn't be long before Crina caught on that she was being drugged. And Iris was running out of time. Her spirit was slipping. She could feel it weakening and withering like the old flowers left in the vases around her house.

The crisping petals made her miss her mom and Gram. If they were there, could they stop Crina? Iris doubted it. Their presence would only put them in danger. Hopefully Aster would make it home. It seemed that she was Iris's only hope. Everyone's only hope. Because there was no way she'd let

Daisy have a face-off with Crina.

Iris's control at hiding her thoughts from Crina was slipping again. She pulled old memories from her mind to keep Crina from knowing what the others were up to.

Why do you always live in the past? Crina sounded irritated, and Iris chose to ignore her.

Crina took Wade's hand in hers and led him up the stairs. Iris could just barely sense the touch of his skin against hers. She longed to hold him. To feel him breathe against her. To nuzzle her nose into his neck and smell the light cologne that was always there.

A few car doors slammed outside. Their guests were arriving.

When they reached her room, Iris felt a release of power. An invisible rope untying from around her. Crina was losing her hold. She draped her arm around Wade's neck and slid her hand into his pocket.

Is that a card in your hand? Panic consumed Iris's thoughts.

Wade noticed she had put something in there, too. Iris wanted to scream for him to stop as his hand went in and he flinched before pulling out the card.

What did you do?

Iris caught a glimpse of the card as Wade brought it up from his pocket. The Death card. He gave her a surprised look before shoving her away from him. "What is this?"

"A tarot card."

NO! Leave him alone. Take it back!

I won't, Crina thought. *He is my final sin. Wrath. He must die so I can live.*

No, no, no, no, NO! Please don't do this. You can't do this.

He extended the card out to her. "Don't you need it for the game?"

She took it from him and tossed it on the bed. "Daisy purchased some other decks. I was trying to pull a joke on you." She flashed him a smile. "You ruined it."

He chuckled, but it wasn't genuine. She knew each of his laughs and smiles and could spot a fake easily. "You should be less obvious next time," he said.

The room spun and Crina swayed. *What did your friends do to me?* she asked, closing her eyes.

Iris could hear the blood rushing through her veins. Her hand came back to her as if it had been frozen and now thawing. She was gaining control of her body. Taking a deep breath, she willed Crina back into the dark corners of her mind.

Wade's smile slipped. "Iris?"

She rubbed her temples. "It's me."

"You okay?" he asked.

"My stomach's woozy." She dropped her hands.

He pulled her into a tight hug. "We had to use more of that stuff Miri made. It's becoming harder to get rid of her."

Voices outside seemed to be multiplying.

Panic fluttered in her chest. "She gave you that card. You're wrath."

"Hey, it's okay. She's gone for now," he said and pressed his lips against her temple. "What do you mean, I'm wrath?"

"To get rid of me completely, she has to hand out cursed cards representing the seven sins." She swallowed back the emotions clogging her throat. "When all of them are finished playing out their fates, I will die. And I think she's going to kill you. She gave you that Death card."

"And I'm wrath?" He backed away. "I don't hate others and I'm not violent. She has it wrong."

"I don't think you are, either. But you have to be careful." She took a step in his direction, placing her hand on his arm. "It doesn't make sense how she twists things. It could be anything."

"We'll just have to get rid of her before anything happens," he said. "Do you know where she put the tarot deck?"

She rushed over to the bed, retrieved the deck from under the mattress, and handed them to him. "There's one problem—"

A sharp pain in her head cut off her words. Her knees thudded to the floor, and the cards slipped out of her hand, spreading across the carpet.

Wade dropped to her side, picked up the deck, and shoved it into the pocket of his lab coat. He brushed the hair from her face. "I won't let you go, Iris. I have to get these to Daisy. We can't wait for Aster." He grabbed the Death card from the bed and darted out of the room.

No. Not Daisy.

Iris watched his departure, tears escaping from her eyes.

Why him? Why wrath?

Crina groaned deeply. *He will do anything for you. How far will he go if someone hurts you?*

Leave him alone. Leave them all alone. Iris was losing command of her arms and legs, becoming a spirit floating inside her own body as Crina retook control.

Chapter Twenty

WADE

The house was dark and empty as Wade came down the stairs. Blue lights traveled across the windows, music and loud voices muffled behind the walls. He went out the back door and into the tent.

He weaved through costumed partiers looking for Daisy. A couple was inside one of his coffins making out. Violet walked the party, making sure no one got too out of hand. Carys and Lauren led the tarot card drinking game. Dena played zombie DJ in the corner. Miri, dressed in an ancient Romanian skirt with a colorful shawl, read cards for people while Daisy assisted her. Wade squeezed his way toward them.

"This party is better than Marsha's," he overhead a girl say to a group. "They even paid that tarot card reader from the boardwalk to do readings."

Good call, Daisy. He had worried about having the older woman at the party. But Daisy had insisted that if they said she was hired, everyone would think it was cool. And she was right.

Daisy spotted him and hurried to meet him.

He leaned over and whispered, "I've got them."

"What?" she yelled over the music.

He pointed to the cards and then to the apartment.

She nodded before following him in there.

"How can anyone hear what Miri is saying in that noise?" he asked, closing the door.

She shrugged and sat on the couch. It used to be the old woman's who had lived here before she died. Tilly was her name. When she was alive, he had helped her a few times. She'd stop him as he headed to the Laynes' back door to visit Iris or pick her up for something. It was either to change a lightbulb in the ceiling fixture or move something heavy so she could vacuum under or behind it. He liked the quirky woman and was sad when she had passed away.

"You okay?" Daisy asked.

"Yeah, just thinking," he said.

The door burst open, letting in the loud music and flashing blue lights. "It's getting crazy out there," Miri said. "Should we go over the plan again?"

They had gone over the plan several times. And several times Miri had asked to clarify them. Was the woman's mind slipping?

"No. I got it down." Daisy looked at Wade. "You?"

"I'm good," Wade said.

"Okay. We need to make room." Miri started to move the chair. Wade took three quick steps to her.

"Let me do that for you." Wade grabbed the chair and slid it out of the way.

Miri sat on the couch next to Daisy.

Wade took out the deck of tarot cards, opened the top, and inserted the Death card, then placed them on the coffee table.

With a smile up at him, Miri removed the cards and placed them on the table in front of Daisy. "Are you ready?"

Daisy eyed the cards. "Maybe we should wait for Aster to get here."

"Her plane was delayed because of the storm in Boston," Wade said.

Miri patted Daisy's knee. "I'll be right here with you. Once you do this, you'll never have to touch the tarot cards again. The sooner we get that spirit out of your sister, the better. She can't hold on much longer."

"Okay, you're right. Let's do this."

"You must practice. Warm up." Miri brought her hand back to her lap. "Pick a card. Don't think about the card, just let your body find the card for you."

Daisy sucked her bottom lip between her teeth and held her hand over the cards.

Someone rapped on the door and the three froze. The startled looks on Daisy's and Miri's faces flew at Wade. Miri covered the tarot cards with her shawl while Wade opened the door.

Dena peeked in her head. "Dude, how's it going? We've been directing people to the house to use the bathroom. Lauren and Carys have started driving some wasted kids home already."

"We're about ready," Wade said. "Have you seen Iris?"

"You won't like this. She's hanging around Josh."

Wade *didn't* like that. He scolded himself for the jealousy raging in his chest. "Keep an eye on her. Don't let her near here and keep her from going off alone with Josh."

"You got it." She closed the door.

Miri carefully lifted up her shawl. "All right, let's give it another try."

Daisy's hand hovered over the tarot cards until she touched one. She screamed as a charge zapped at her fingertips and a flash of light filled the room. The cards flew up before falling around Daisy and Miri.

"What was that?" Daisy held her hand against her chest.

Miri's gaze went from the cards to Daisy. "I'm not sure. When Aster touched the cards, there wasn't a shock like that. The cards must be broken."

"Broken?" Daisy blew on her hurt fingertips.

Miri glanced at Wade. "Are you sure all the cards are here?"

"Not sure," Wade said. "I just took the box and the card Crina gave me."

Miri nodded, her eyes surveying the cards scattered around her and Daisy. "We need to make certain they all are accounted for. Help me pick them up."

Daisy hesitated before touching the cards.

"You sit back, dear," Miri said. "Wade and I can get them."

After the cards were gathered, Miri started stacking them in five piles.

Wade opened and closed his hands into fists, pacing. He wanted to be with Iris and worried about Josh being at the party. The thing was, he was also concerned about leaving Daisy alone with Miri. The old woman didn't look able to defend herself, let alone both of them.

He wasn't sure about this magic thing or that it was safe for Daisy. From what he'd heard, Aster could kill people with fate changing. He glanced at Miri. She paused stacking the cards and patted Daisy's hand, whispering something to her. It seemed like the older woman was comforting Daisy.

Miri's eyes turned to Wade. "I won't let anything happen to her."

Wade nodded and combed his fingers through his hair. "So what are the piles for?"

The next card she placed on the pile slapped against the top one. "I'm separating them into five groups. This one is the Major Arcanas, then these"—she tapped the other four stacks— "the minor ones in suits—wands, pentacles, swords, and cups. We should have a total of seventy-eight cards."

The slapping of the cards was the only noise in the room, except for the blaring of music and voices outside thrumming against the walls. Daisy stared at her hands as if she was trying to will them to stop shaking.

"One's missing," Miri said, counting the cards of one stack. "A Major Arcana. The Tower card." She looked up at Wade. "Maybe one was dropped on your way here? Or left in Iris's room?"

He opened the door. "I'll go search for it. Stay here. Keep the door locked and only open it for me."

"We will," Miri said. "Daisy and I will be fine. We can finish moving the furniture out of the way for the exorcism."

Daisy's head popped up. "Wait. What? An exorcism? I'm going to do one of those?"

"For lack of a better word, yes," Miri said. "But you needn't worry. I will be with you the entire time."

"Hey," Wade said. "Look at me, Dais."

She looked at him with scared eyes.

"I'm with you. We got this," Wade said. She smiled slightly and nodded at him.

"Don't forget to lock this." He shut the door.

Wade snaked his way around the partiers who all seemed to be getting more inebriated by the minute. Violet met him before he had made it halfway through the tent.

She grabbed his arm and leaned into him. "What's going on?"

"We're missing a tarot card," he said. "Have you seen Iris around?"

"In that corner." She nodded in the direction. "With Josh. I don't like this."

Iris was sitting close to Josh, using all her best flirt moves, but there was something different to them. Less cute. More seductive. He pushed down his jealousy. "Well, at least he's keeping her busy," he said. "Any signs of Iris coming back?"

"No," she said. "And she hasn't been drinking any punch. I stopped offering her some because I think she's getting suspicious."

Wade decided it was time to play the boyfriend card. "Stay around Dena. Don't go off on your own."

He went inside to the kitchen and searched the refrigerator. On the bottom shelf, he found what he was looking for. A Dr Pepper. He grabbed the can and went back to the tent. He found Violet with Dena by the DJ stand, their heads close together as Violet whispered in Dena's ear.

"I need some of those drops," Wade said, cracking open the can. He positioned his body to block Iris's view as Violet emptied a dropperful of Miri's concoction into the Dr Pepper. "Let's hope this works," he said.

"Oh, we're praying, all right," Dena said. "That we don't all get killed."

Wade ignored her and strode over to where Iris was practically sitting on Josh's lap. "Hey," he said. "Here you are. I've been looking all over for you."

"You haven't been looking that hard," Iris said, laughing. "I've been right here most of the night. Isn't that right, Josh?"

Wade wasn't sure what the drops would do to him, but he had to make her think the Dr Pepper was safe to drink. He took a sip. Iris couldn't resist the drink, and he was hoping the evil spirit in her would want it, too.

"I should leave you two alone to talk," Josh said, standing.

"Yes, you should." Wade glared, acting every bit the jealous boyfriend. Which he was. He hated seeing Josh so close to Iris. Even if it wasn't really her, it was her body.

"I'll see you later," Josh said and walked off.

Wade sat beside Iris. "What are you doing? I thought we

were together." He had to keep up the show. He didn't offer the drink. If he knew Iris, she'd ask him for it. But there was no telling what this spirit would do.

"Did we ever say we were together?" She grabbed the can from him and took a long drink.

Wade struggled to keep from smiling. Apparently, unlike Iris, the spirit was rude. "I guess we haven't." He pushed to his feet. "Feel free to do whatever you want."

She grabbed his hand, stopping him from walking off. "Are you mad at me?"

Josh hovered nearby, waiting for his chance to get back with Iris.

Wade pulled his hand away. "I'm going to get another soda."

"Don't be too long," she said.

When he exited the tent and was out of view of Iris, he bounded up the porch steps, through the house, and up the stairs to Iris's room. He searched the mattress for the Tower card. It wasn't there. He looked under the bed and sorted through the clothes and magazines left on the comforter. Still nothing. And it wasn't on or under the window seat cushion. Not on the dresser or nightstand. Nowhere. He heard steps approaching and quickly stretched out on the bed.

Iris opened the door and glanced around the room as she entered. "What are you doing in here?"

"I needed quiet." He sat up. "Why did you leave your boyfriend?"

She frowned at him and sat beside him on the bed. "Come on. You know I only have eyes for you."

"Obviously."

"Are you being sarcastic?"

"Glad you noticed." Wade wished the drops would work already. He wanted Iris back. The spirit's personality was ugly. Iris was so much more than that.

She pushed him back against the pillows and straddled him. "I can make it up to you."

"Not interested." He lifted her off him and put her on the bed beside him.

"If you're not, I know someone who would be." She swung her legs over the side of the bed.

He grabbed her hand before she could leave. "You don't want to get messed up with Josh."

She yanked her hand away. "On the contrary, I bet he would be fun to *get messed up with*."

On the contrary? The words she used reminded Wade that she wasn't Iris.

Before she reached the door, she rocked on her feet. She gasped and dropped to her knees, clenching her head.

Wade was at her side in an instant. His pulse raced. Fear that something was wrong with her rocked his insides. He lifted her in his arms and carried her to the bed, gently placing her on the mattress. Her hand was cold when he held it. "Iris?"

Her eyes opened. "Wade?"

He wasn't sure if it was Iris or the spirit. "Remember that day we met? During volleyball."

"Yes," she said and sat up. "Of course I do. It's me, Wade. Besides, she can search my memories. So your test won't work. The ball was yellow."

He blinked at her.

"That's what you were going to ask me, right?"

"Yes," he said. "I'm that predictable, am I?"

"You are." She stood, her balance a little wobbly. "The Dr Pepper was a great idea. Violet's been pushing that punch all night. But Crina wanted to stay alert and not get drunk, so she wouldn't have any of it."

"Crina?"

"That's the spirit's name." Tears formed in her eyes. "She was the one who cursed Reese's family. The crazy part is that she's from my grandfather's family line. Obviously she doesn't care about family bonds. I don't know how she's planning it, but she wants you and Josh to get into a fight."

Wade towed her into his arms and held her as she cried.

She clung to him. "I'm so scared."

"We're going to stop her."

"How will we do that?"

"I can't tell you. If you know, she could find out." He pulled away to look in her eyes. They glistened against the bedroom lights like sunrays on blue water. He hated to see her suffer. And she had been suffering. Struggling with the evil spirit inside her.

"I know," she whispered. "I'm just so tired. I want to sleep."

Wade took her back to the bed and helped her lay down. "Do you know where the Tower card is? We have the deck, but that one is missing."

"Crina gave it to Josh. She said he was going to fall from his tower." She grabbed his arm. "You have to be careful. She wants to kill you."

He touched her cheek. "I know. I'll be fine. Don't worry. You rest here. We can't have her coming out and discovering what we're up to. You can see and hear us when she's taken over, right?"

"Yes. Why?"

"And she can't, am I right?"

"Right. I think I can because I'm the host. She mentioned she goes to sleep or something. But she can tap into my memories like I can hers. I think she's been too busy to look into them tonight, though."

Wade kissed her soft, pale lips and pulled her throw blanket over her. "You rest. I'll be back as soon as I can."

Wade pounded down the stairs, slipping slightly on the final step. He righted himself and stormed out the back door into the tent. Carys stopped him just after he entered.

"There's something fishy going on with Lauren and Josh," she said. "I've found them whispering to each other a few times, and when they spotted me, they immediately stopped talking and moved away from each other."

"That is fishy." He glanced around the party. The flashing blue light annoyed the shit out of him. "Keep an eye on Lauren. Have you seen Josh?"

"Yes. He's over there." She pointed to the other side of the room.

The tent reeked of alcohol and sweaty bodies. Costume makeup dripped from drenched faces, their owners dancing. Masks had been discarded or pushed up on top of heads. As he passed the punch bowl, he noticed it was almost empty.

Josh's back was turned when he came up to him. "I need to talk to you," Wade said.

With a sharp laugh, Josh spun around, a stupid smile on his face. "She was my girlfriend first. If anyone should be mad, it's me. Don't get so upset. We were only flirting."

"We both know you're afraid of me. You remember what I did to you last time. I won't ruin that pretty face of yours, if…" Wade paused for effect. The last time they fought, Josh and a few of his friends had jumped him. Wade was the only one left standing.

"If what?" There was fear in Josh's eyes.

Wade smiled. "Iris gave you a tarot card. I want it."

Confusion crossed his face. "Why would you want that?"

"It's an old family heirloom," Wade lied.

Josh reached into his pocket, pulled out the card, and handed it to him.

Wade took it. "Good. Stay away from Iris." He passed Carys as he rushed to the apartment door.

Carys trailed him. "Lauren told me that Josh was asking questions about Iris and you. She thinks he's up to something.

He told her that Iris made a play for him and he was going to meet her upstairs."

"Shit." Wade seethed and darted a look over his shoulder. Josh was where Wade had left him. He knocked hard on the door. "It's Wade," he called.

Miri opened it for him. "I have the card," he said, passing it to her. Carys followed him in.

Daisy and Miri had moved the furniture against the wall while he was gone. The hatbox sat on the floor beside Daisy.

"So how does this work?" he asked.

"Let's see if Daisy can claim the cards," Miri said, struggling to sit down on the carpet opposite Daisy. "Are you ready, dear?"

"I guess so," said Daisy, sitting pretzel-style and wringing her hands.

Miri shuffled the tarot cards and glimpsed up at Wade. "She has to change someone's fate. Do you care to volunteer?"

Wade didn't like the idea. After hearing everything changing fates had done to the Layne family, he wasn't too thrilled about having his changed. Wade gave Carys a sidelong glance.

"Violet told me about the fate changing. I'll do it," Carys said, kneeling in front of Miri.

Miri laid the cards out on the floor in what she called a Celtic cross. She flipped over each card, explaining their meanings and telling Carys how they pertained to her.

When one of the cards fell with the image upside down from the rest, Miri stopped. "The Ace of Cups reversed," she said. "It means you feel drained. As though recent events have sucked the life out of you." With her eyes on Daisy, she nodded at the card. "Go ahead. Touch it."

Daisy placed her fingertips on the card. A spark zapped at her hand, and the card flew up into the air. Two spinning hologram images of the Ace card separated from the original.

They spun in different directions before they stopped and each turned the opposite way they had been going before. The images slapped back together and the card dropped to the floor.

"You've claimed the cards." Miri took Daisy's hand in hers and turned it over. On Daisy's wrist was the shape of an infinity symbol glowing red. "The fate has changed," Miri said.

"I'm feeling better already," Carys said.

Miri gave her a warm smile. "You're a good girl. I can see it in your cards."

"Yeah," Wade said. "It's not your fault Dena texted you that pic and Marsha saw it on your phone."

Carys lowered her head, pulling a carpet fiber that was longer than the rest. "Thanks. I really felt bad about it."

Miri rolled onto her knees and struggled to her feet. "Now, we just need Iris to do the ritual."

Wade headed for the door. "Okay, I'll get her."

His mind was foggy as he left the small apartment. Magic did exist. He'd seen it, but how would he know Carys's fate had been changed? That couldn't be seen. It had to play out, and he wouldn't know for sure until it did.

And what about Iris? There was no way to know for sure if their plan would work. But they had to try. For tonight, he had to believe in magic. It was Iris's only hope.

Chapter Twenty-One

Iris/Crina

Teen girls in this time were shallow beings. They stressed more about what to wear and how popular they were than was necessary. Crina never had that luxury of worrying about frivolous things. If they'd lived in the eighteenth century, they'd be worried more about finding their next meal than about which color of the rainbow to dye their hair.

And Crina was determined to live that easy life.

What did she care that an innocent girl died? Death came easily in the time Crina was born. She was used to it. After witnessing many deaths, she had become numb to it. Hadn't even cried when a disease took her younger brother. Iris had lived long if one were to think of it in terms of Crina's life span. She had died at nearly sixteen.

Crina fixed her hair in the mirror. "Iris, why are you hiding up here when there is a party going on? Maybe you would like some company?" She picked up Iris's phone and texted Josh to come up to her room. The Dr Pepper must've diluted the drops, and Crina might not have gotten enough of the potion, because for the last thirty minutes, Iris and Crina were trading places frequently.

The mirror warped and the room darkened. "Crap. Not now." Crina braced her hands on the dresser. "You're starting to annoy me, Iris."

Iris took several calming breaths to get past the headache that always preceded the change. When she had complete control of her body again, she kicked off her shoes, yanked open her bedroom door, and darted down the hall. The stairs squeaked below her and she thudded to a stop.

Oh no. Josh.

She stood there for several quick beats, listening.

It could be Wade.

Then she realized she was in the open. There was no way she wanted to confront Josh. He wasn't coming to her room to talk. Crina had made it clear she wanted to go all the way with him.

Iris scrambled down the hall in the opposite direction of the stairs. She opened the glass door and stepped out onto the balcony. The wind whipped her hair around her face and sent chills across her skin. The headache was coming on again.

Crina took control so easily that Iris knew the drops were wearing off. "Why are you running from him? I will win in the end."

Iris wasn't going down without a fight. She pushed to take control.

Crina opened the door, locked it from the inside, and shut it, trapping them on the balcony. She sent a text to Josh that she was on the balcony and tossed the phone over the banister before Iris took over again.

Iris tried the knob, but the door was locked. She was stuck without a phone. No way to call for help. The balcony was small and crowded with a chaise chair, tiny table, and a tiki torch attached to a stand. Her grandfather wanted a place to have his coffee and look out at the ocean from this height. Gram Froggatt's house was on the ledge of a cliff. The beach below sent sounds of the ocean rolling over her.

Iris thought of climbing over the balcony and shimmying on the ledge to the closest window, but it was a long way down. And she didn't like heights. She gripped the railing, and it shook a little. One of the bolts connecting to the wall was stripped. Her grandfather had meant to fix it, but he never got around to doing it. Gram hardly ever came out here. No one in the family really had since Gramps's passing. Iris would sit on his chaise chair when she missed him. It smelled like the cigars he smoked out there and a little like the aloe oil he rubbed on his skin.

The doorknob behind her rattled, then unlocked.

Josh stepped out onto the balcony. "Are we playing hide-and-seek? I do like to play games."

Iris backed away from him. "Leave me alone."

"I don't understand. You asked me to come here." He stepped up to her. Alcohol hinted on his breath. "I remember coming out here during parties. We'd want to find a place to be alone. Of course, those were your mother's parties. A lot less wild than this one."

He placed his open hand on her cheek, and she moved her head away from him.

"You're playing hard to get. Trying to tease me?" He stepped closer, pushing her up against the railing. "You want me to work for it, huh?"

Iris pushed on his chest, but he barely budged. "Go away, Josh. It was a mistake. Someone else had my phone. I didn't send those texts."

"That's not what you said at school," he said. "You wanted to make sure I brought condoms. I've been looking forward to this since you mentioned it."

Where was Crina now? She wasn't trying to come out. This was her plan. She wanted Iris to be present for this. Then what? Play out the curse she gave Josh. She set this up to complete his fate. Iris thought of the tarot card she'd given him. The Tower card.

The image on the card was a tower on fire with a man and woman falling down its side. She glanced over her shoulder. The living room light was on now, and she could see the jagged rocks on the ground below.

"Josh, we should go inside."

"Iris!" Wade called from the hall.

She started to scream, and Josh's hand flew to her mouth, muffling it. He wrapped his arm tightly around her. She struggled in his grip, his hand firm on her mouth.

"Why are you doing this?" he hissed against her ear. "You can't just keep playing us, Iris. Going from me to Wade."

She bit his hand.

"Ouch!" He backed away from her. "What the hell, Iris?"

"What the hell?" she repeated. "I've changed my mind. I don't want anything to do with you. Ever! And when a girl says no, you need to understand she means it." She tried to push by him, but he cut her off, backing her up against the railing again. "Let me go, Josh. You've been drinking. You don't want to do this."

"From the first time we met, I had to have you." He kissed her neck.

She leaned away from him to get his lips off her, glancing over the balcony. Her stomach twisted. It was so far down to the rocks below that if he pushed too hard, she wouldn't survive the fall.

She turned her head and stared into his eyes. "Let me go, Josh. *Please.*"

He didn't budge, so she kicked at his shins and stomped his foot. "Ow," he seethed.

His grip loosened, and Iris wiggled away from him. She ran for the door, but he caught her arm. With all her might, she tugged it away from him. He stumbled back against the railing and it gave way, one side still clinging to the wall.

"Help!" Josh yelled. His hands squeezed the railing as he hung there kicking his feet and trying to get a footing on anything.

Iris scrambled over to the edge. If she reached her hand to help him, his weight could pull her over with him. She had to get help, so she stumbled to her feet.

"Don't leave me!" Josh hollered.

"I have to get help," she said. "Hang on."

"I can't. My hands are slipping." His voice sounded panicked, and his hand slid down the railing. He was moving too far away from the ledge.

"Help!" Iris screamed, searching for something that would reach him. She spotted the tiki torch and dragged it across the deck floor. Easing to the edge, she held the stand and reached the torch part out to him. "Grab it!" And she yelled one more, "Help!"

He caught the torch with one hand while the other still held the railing. Oil from the top of the torch sprayed his face. "Shit. What is that?"

"Forget that and hold on." She braced her feet on the deck, digging her toes into a crack. Like rowing a boat, she pulled him up an inch or so at a time until he was able to gain footing on the railing.

Her arms and palms burned. Just as her hold slipped, two strong hands joined hers on the pole. They pulled again, and Josh was able to swing his leg onto the balcony.

"Keep a hold on it," Wade ordered before letting go of the pole. He held his hand out and Josh grasped it.

"Thank you," Josh said, breathless. His foot rolled over some debris from the wall and he lost his balance, falling back. Wade grabbed Josh's arm, and the two fell back over the ledge.

"OMIGOD! NO!" Iris dropped to her knees.

They both held onto the railing, the remaining bolts straining from their weight. Josh's grip on the railing was closer to the balcony. She had to help him, but she worried Wade wouldn't be able to hold on that long.

The Death card.

This has been amusing to watch. Crina's laugh in Iris's head grated against her brain. *Such a comedy of errors.*

Anger rose in Iris, and she strangled Crina out of her thoughts. She gripped Josh's arms and helped him up. He rolled on his back, catching his breath for a second before getting to his feet.

He searched the balcony. "Where's the torch?"

Iris glanced around. It wasn't there. "It must've fallen off."

Wade clung to the railing, too far away for her to reach him. "Don't let go." Her fear sounded in her voice.

"I'm trying," Wade said, clenching his teeth.

Josh squeezed her shoulder. "I have to find something. Keep talking to him."

Iris nodded, tears dripping from her nose. "Okay, hurry."

Before he left, Violet burst through the door. "What's happening here?"

"Help them," Josh said, pushing by her.

"Violet." Fear sounded in Iris's voice. She needed to be strong for Wade. "Crina gave him the Death card. She gave him…"

Violet stared at Wade for a quick second, and then she darted out the door.

"Where are you going? Violet! I need your help. Don't leave!" She cried so hard she shook. "Don't leave," she barely whispered, lowering her head.

"Look at me, Iris," Wade said.

Iris lifted her head.

"I'm okay," he said.

The bolt loosened from the wall, barely holding the railing. It caused Wade's arm to yank, but he held on. She darted looks over her shoulder, wondering what was taking Josh so long. Just when she was giving up hope, Josh returned with a bedsheet.

Josh tied knots in it before lowering it down. Wade took his right hand off the railing and reached for the sheet. A gust of wind blew the sheet away from his hand and Wade swung back.

"Hold on!" Iris's voice was rough and hardly any noise came out. The wind circled her, and it was as if a million pins pricked her at once. She fell back gasping, turning her head to see Wade. Something burned inside Iris, and she reached out to Wade, her hand falling limp against the decking.

The curses! Iris heard Crina scream. *They're back. How are they back?* It was as if Iris had left her body, watching as Wade gripped the sheet and Josh pulled him up.

He's okay. Iris willed her body to move. She desperately wanted to go to him, but no matter how hard she tried to get up, she couldn't.

How is he alive? Crina asked.

You lose, was Iris's last thought.

Chapter Twenty-Two

WADE

Wade gasped for air. He was alive. His muscles ached; even the tips of his fingers burned. He rolled his head to the side. A few feet away from him, Iris was motionless, her eyes wide as she stared at him.

He twisted around and struggled to his knees.

Josh shot his hand out to him. "Dude, you okay?"

Wade raised his head. There was something in Josh's eyes. Relief? Wade took Josh's hand and he towed him up. "Thanks, man."

Violet came rushing out the door onto the balcony. She glanced around, and at noticing Iris still lying on the balcony, she dropped to her knees beside her and took her face in her hands. "Are you okay?"

Iris nodded against her hands.

"Daisy did it," Violet said. "There was an entry in those notebooks by a woman named Dika. That spirit had cursed her, too. She wrote how to stop cursed tarot cards. Daisy changed everyone's fate and the curse went back to the spirit." She looked at Wade, then back at Iris. "It has a ritual to exorcize that demon bitch from you. We need to get you to Daisy."

Iris pushed herself up to her feet. "Let's go." She sounded strange to Wade. Something was different in the tone of her voice. Her eyes darting around at the faces in front of her, she backed up to the opened door. "I won't let you send me away. If you try to rid Iris of me, I will take her with me." Wade made his move for her. She slammed the door before he could reach her and locked it, trapping him with Violet and Josh on the balcony.

Wade turned the knob frantically. "Shit. We have to get out of here. She's going to do something to Iris."

Josh tried the window by the door that led into the house. "Locked," he said.

Violet picked up a tiny wrought-iron table by the chaise chair and slammed it against the window. The window shattered with a crash, glass spilling to the wooden deck. Josh wrapped the sheet around his arm and brushed away the jagged pieces clinging to the window frame. After draping the sheet over the sill, he climbed inside and unlocked the door.

"What fucked-up game are you guys playing? You could have killed me!" Josh stormed down the hall.

"I swear that guy is going to get his one day." Wade pushed by Violet. "Come on, we have to find Iris. Do you know where she'd go?"

"It's not Iris. I don't have a clue where Crina would go," Violet said from behind Wade, the sound of her hurried steps following him.

Wade glanced over his shoulder. "Text Dena and ask her if she's seen Iris, or have her search for her. Maybe Carys and Lauren can help."

When they got to the tent, they watched Josh get into his

car and speed away. If there were justice, he'd get pulled over.

"We need to clear out the party," Violet yelled over the music.

"Can't now," he said, breathing like a bull through his nose. "The police will detain us. Ask questions. That spirit could hurt Iris while we're held up."

"Who is it?" Miri's voice came from the other side of the door.

"It's us. Violet and Wade," she yelled.

The door eased open and Wade pushed on it, too anxious to wait. "Is Iris here?"

"No," Miri said. "We haven't seen her."

Wade looked past Miri at Daisy. She was sitting on the floor with cards perfectly aligned in a partially formed circle around her. One card was pinched between her fingers. Her eyes closed, she nodded and placed the card next to the others.

"What is she doing?" Wade asked.

Miri's eyes went to where Wade's were staring. "She's feeling the cards. It's like a puzzle. Each fate changer has her own pattern for an exorcism. Once the circle is closed, we must get Iris in the middle. Then Daisy will complete the ritual by touching the main card."

Sweat dripped from Wade's forehead and he wiped it away with his sleeve. He hadn't realized how overheated he was. "And that's going to work?"

"We can hope," she said. "It was in Dika's notes."

"We'll find Iris," he said. "Keep the door locked and don't let her in. Even if she says she's Iris. We can't trust that spirit. I don't want you alone with her."

Wade shut the door and the locks slid into place.

"What do we do?" Violet asked, eyes frantically searching the party. "Where did she go?"

"She must know that we need her to complete that ritual."

Violet turned to him. "I'll check here. The house. Garage."

Dena and Carys approached, maneuvering around partiers.

"No. We stick together." Wade tugged his phone out of his pocket. He sent a text to Iris, hoping she had her phone. "You come with me. Dena and Carys can search here. "Where are we going?"

"The beach and the rock jetties." He walked off, meeting Dena and Carys by the punch bowl. He wanted all the partiers gone. He was sure that spirit was going to fight them, and he didn't want anyone asking questions or thinking they were attacking Iris.

The wind bit at Wade's exposed skin. His lab coat didn't offer much warmth. He pulled up the collar and tread across the beach. The smell of seaweed was strong and the lapping of waves was a welcoming sound to the loud party he'd just left. Violet kept brushing her hair from her eyes. The light from the flashlight in her trembling hand danced over the sand.

"How is this even happening?" he asked. "I've been trying to wrap my mind around it and I just can't. It's so fucking crazy."

Violet glanced down at her shoes. "I've told you everything, but I understand. It was tough for me, as well." She looked over at him. "But we can do this. Once we find Iris, we can end all the crazy and get rid of those stupid cards."

Wade heaved a sigh. "I'm going to need a shrink after this is all done."

"Tell me about it." She laughed—a quiet, sarcastic one. "I'm seeing a therapist. It helps. But I can't really tell her why I need her help. We just deal with my attempted suicide."

"I'm sorry," he said.

"No need to be. I'm fine."

"I'm glad you're here."

"Where is she?" Violet's voice was shaky as she changed the subject.

Fear sank in his stomach, wondering what that spirit would do to the girl he loved. Would she harm Iris? He used the flashlight to see the shore, hitting the whitecaps on the waves. The rock jetty looked like a dead body stretching out from the beach into the ocean. Water hit the base of the rocks and sprayed up in the air.

Violet abruptly stopped, a gasp escaping from her lips.

Wade's eyes followed the stream of light coming from her flashlight. It caught something in the distance. Iris jumped from rock to rock on the rock mound, heading for the ocean. Wade didn't say anything. He sprinted across the beach toward the jetty.

"She's going to jump," Violet called after him, the beam of light bouncing sporadically as she ran after him.

He climbed the first rock, and then moved as quickly as possible across them. His boot slid on a slick one, and he crashed down on his knees and elbows, the pain rocking his bones. He slipped a little as he got to his feet. He had to keep going. Save Iris. Her silhouette was a ghostly figure against the dark sky and ocean. Violet's light swept across Iris. He was almost there.

Almost.

Three steps.

And she jumped.

"Iris!" he yelled, diving in after her. It was as if a million icy knives stabbed him. The ocean's frozen embrace engulfed him. He couldn't see her. Where was she? It was too dark. Seaweed tangled in his arms. He pulled from them and moved farther out. "Iris!" he called again, gulping in water, the salt burning his throat.

She was gone.

Gone!

Panic hit his chest with thundering beats. His arms and legs ached as he rose and fell with the waves.

I can't lose her.

He dived under, reaching, searching for her. His breath ran out and he broke through the waves, bobbing and sucking in air and water.

Where is she?

"Wade!" Was it Violet calling out? He spun around, riding a wave, and crashed against a rock. Pain erupted in his side.

He pushed off the rock and swam a ways out.

"Wade!" There was a frightened shriek in the voice.

He turned to look at the jetty. Violet flashed her light over the water and pointed. "She's there!"

"Wade!" Another terrified scream. It was Iris calling him.

He swam to her, coming up behind her and wrapping his arm around her chest. "Stay still. I have you." He pushed through the water with his legs and free arm, dragging her toward the beach. When he could stand, he lifted her into his arms and carried her out.

The beam from the flashlight bounced across the jetty's rocks as Violet made her way across to them. He laid Iris on the sand and she rolled to her side, coughing up water. Each breath he took hurt and he touched his side. Blood drenched his fingers.

Sand kicked up around him as Violet reached them and fell to her knees.

"Is she okay?"

"Yeah," he said, nodding, still straining to breathe.

"What happened?" Iris said through coughs and tears. At least, he thought it was her. She rolled onto her back.

"Crina tried to kill you," Violet said and lifted Iris's head on her lap. She brushed the wet strands of hair from her sister's face. "It is you, right?"

"Yes."

"What's my favorite dessert?"

"Really?" Iris got to her elbows. "It changes all the time."

Violet laughed. "Yes, it does."

Wade stood and looked down at Iris. "We have to bring you to Daisy. Can you get up?"

"I think so," she said.

He took her hands and helped her stand. His side protested and he winced, but he wouldn't let go of Iris's right hand.

Violet pointed the flashlight at him. "You're bleeding."

"I'm fine. Come on."

Iris pulled her hand away from him, backing up. "Leave me alone," she ordered, falling to the sand on her butt and scooting away from them. Her hand came across a piece of driftwood and she grasped.

Wade took an uncertain step forward. "We're trying to help you."

She tottered to her feet and held out the branch. "Don't come any closer or I'll hit you."

"Crina?" He cautiously slid his foot in the sand, moving closer.

"You do not understand," she said, swinging the branch back and forth. "I will not go back. Not there. Evil is there. I am not the only spirit in those cards. It is full of firstborns. Those stolen from the curse. They torment me."

"You can't have Iris." Another step and Wade could grab her. He had to get her back to Daisy. Stop this crazy messed-up stuff. Shoving the hopelessness aside, he moved forward. Seeing her scared and hurt tore at him.

I'll do whatever it takes to save you, Iris. Just hold tight. Daisy and Miri were his only chance to get Iris back. No matter the cost to him.

Crina swung her weapon at him again. "What would you do if it were you?" she asked. Her tortured expression made Wade want to hold her, take on whatever demon held her. Anything to remove her pain. "I am not an evil person," she said. "I am a girl who made a foolish mistake. Am I to suffer eternity for it?"

Violet moved to Wade's side. "We could find a way to release you. There has to be something we can do."

"Stop trying to trick me." Crina backed away, her hcels sinking in the sand. Her wet dress stuck to her skin and her water-drenched hair slapped her face as she turned her head back and forth to watch them and then her steps.

Violet heaved a long sigh and glanced at Wade. "Just knock her out."

He shot a puzzled look at her. "What?"

"Deck her. We don't have time for this."

There was no way he could hit a girl, even if it was a demon spirit instead of Iris. It was her body. "I can't."

Crina glared at him. "You are such a weak man."

Violet rushed Crina and punched her square on the jaw with so much force both girls stumbled back. "Ouch," Violet groaned.

Crina, her shoes stuck in the sand, lost her balance and fell right on her butt.

Wade grabbed her arms and lifted her over his shoulder.

"Put me down," Crina screeched.

"Come on," he told Violet as he trudged through the sand with Crina kicking and beating her fists against his back.

Everything on his body hurt and real blood covered his chest, but he was saving Iris, damn it.

Chapter Twenty-Three

Iris/Crina

The pressure against her stomach from Wade's shoulder made Crina want to get sick all over his back. She had to think. Get herself out of this situation. Her jaw hurt from Violet's punch and she vowed to get even.

Just let me go. Iris felt like a wisp of smoke. She could barely think anymore, let alone fight Crina for control. *You're a murderer. Your curse killed all those first-born sons. You will rot in hell.*

Cease your jabbering. Crina's thoughts were strong and angry.

Iris held onto whatever energy she had left. *Or maybe this IS your hell.*

"I *said* stop! Get out of my head." Crina squirmed, twisting her body, her fists thudding against Wade's wet back.

"Iris? Keep fighting her." Wade's voice boomed through her thoughts like an overhead speaker. Iris wanted desperately to touch him, but Crina had control and Iris couldn't feel a thing. It was like having her head, arms, and legs strapped to a gurney. No matter how hard she tried to make a body part move, it wouldn't budge.

But Crina had no problems moving. She kicked and punched Wade until her foot connected with his hurt side and he dropped her. She landed hard, her head and back smacking against the deck.

"Crap," he seethed.

The pain caused stars to flash against Iris's eyelids. She was back. "Wade, hurry. She's gone. Get me to Daisy." She sat up. Her stomach turned, bile burning her throat. Tears stung her eyes and tumbled down her cheeks.

Violet helped Iris to her feet and wrapped Iris's arm over her shoulder for support. "We got this. Right?"

Iris's eyes met Violet's gaze. "My head. I can't… She's too strong."

"No, she isn't," Violet protested. "You keep coming back. Fighting her. If she were too strong, you wouldn't be here. So, come on. Man up."

"Okay." Iris sounded anything but strong. She shivered against the cold. Her wet hair stuck like ice on her face. But she forced a smile for her sister. *Put on a brave face*, Gram would tell her. She'd been saying that ever since Josh and his friends started bullying her at school.

Your hold is waning. Crina broke through her foggy mind.

Wade held his side and staggered over. He was soaking wet. "Let's get this done before that psycho returns."

It was like shards of glass sliced at her head with each step up the deck stairs to the house. Some party stragglers teetered down the driveway waiting for Ubers. Dena kept herding the few leftovers to the entry as Lauren aided a girl out of the tent. Carys held a green trash bag as she picked up red cups and other garbage.

"What happened to you guys?" Carys looked pointedly

at Wade. "Were you in a knife fight?"

Dena pushed on a guy's back. "Come on, dude. Keep moving." The guy walked as if he were on a moving train. She stopped in front of Wade. "Oh gosh, you're drenched."

"Can you grab some sweats from Iris's room?" Violet asked her.

"What about Wade? I'm sure your stuff won't fit him."

Violet glanced over him as though she was assessing his size. "My dad has stuff in the guest room."

"Will do." Dena jogged off for the house.

Violet guided Iris to the apartment beside the garage. Miri let them in and helped Violet cover Iris and Wade with beach towels from the storage bins by the door. Iris sat on the couch. She was so cold her teeth rattled against each other. Her head was silent. Was Crina gone? Maybe the cold was the key to keeping her away.

Violet kneeled down in front of Iris, rubbing her arms. "We must get you warm. You could get hypothermia." She glanced at the door. "Where is Dena?"

Iris half listened as Wade told Miri and Daisy what had happened on the beach. Her fingers were still pale and like raisins at the tips. Her jaw hurt and she remembered it was from Violet's punch only when Wade mentioned it.

Dena barged in with clothes, and Violet took Iris into the bathroom to change. The thick makeup Crina had put on Iris was almost gone. Mascara and eyeliner ran from her eyes like black rivers. Hints of glitter reflected in the harsh lights over the mirror. Iris struggled out of the wet costume and into her sweatpants, T-shirt, and hoodie.

The scent of fabric softener sheets on the clothes comforted her. Laundry and baking smells always made her think of Gram. She wanted her gram so hard right then. Everything always seemed okay when she was around. She pulled some tissues from a box on the sink and wiped as much of the black smudge away from her eyes.

A knock came from the door. "Hurry up," Wade said. "What's taking so long?"

Violet opened the door.

"Daisy is almost ready," he said.

Violet came up behind Iris and gathered her hair into a loose bun, securing it with a hair tie.

Iris stared at her sister's reflection in the mirror. They were like matching shoes, except one was a size bigger than the other. Growing up, she never had to ask Violet how she felt. And Violet never had to ask her. But ever since Aster messed with their fates, they'd become strangers. When all this was over, Iris would do whatever it took to get back to how they were before.

Wade peered in through the crack of the door. "This isn't prom. We have to do this now."

Violet nodded and stepped out of the bathroom. Iris followed her, but Wade stopped her, cupping her face in his hands.

"Whatever happens," he said. "You know...I'm here for you. I'll do everything I can to get you back." Everything he felt was in those beautiful dark eyes of his, and the love there burned through her. She held back her tears, wanting to stay strong for him. Needing to stay strong for herself, too. She choked on a sob.

"I love you, Iris. Always have." He kissed her, his lips firm and warm on hers. It was a kiss filled with hope and desperation. And fear of losing her? Because she was afraid of being lost. "I love you," he whispered against her lips this time.

He loves me. Her heart ached and soared at the same time. She needed to hear those three words from him. But the evil waiting inside her head, waiting for her turn to take over, made them bittersweet. His lips left hers, and she leaned into his embrace.

She swallowed hard. "I love you."

He lifted her chin with cold fingers. "You have been my entire world for so long. My strength. Every memory worth remembering for the past five years includes you. I've missed you so much. I can't lose you now. Fight. For me. For your family. But most of all, for you. Promise me you won't give up."

She nodded against his fingers. "I promise."

He kissed her again, with that tender desperation. It was too quick. When he pulled away, an instant cold shivered across her lips.

"Let's get that spirit out of you," he said, taking her hand and leading her to where Daisy stood in front of a circle of perfectly aligned tarot cards. Miri was by a table of lit candles.

How sweet. Did you forget I was here? Crina sounded angry as she pushed against Iris. Iris's heart fluttered fast in her chest, and she swore a stroke was coming on. That familiar numbness overcame her and the sense of Wade's hand squeezing hers faded.

"Get in the circle," Daisy said.

A spark rushed over Crina as she gained control of Iris. She let go of Wade's hand and slowly crossed the wooden floor. She needed a distraction.

The outside world was slipping away from Iris. She was too weak, and with it came an intense pain. A feeling of loss. She would never see Mom and Dad, Gram, her sisters, or Wade again. There was so much she wanted to say to them. Things she should've said every day. *I love you.*

Just die already, Crina thought. *You're causing me to lose my concentration.*

You can't win, Crina. They won't let you. We can find a way to help you. Iris was reaching for anything to stop Crina.

I am truly sorry. Crina's thoughts sounded sincere. *If there were another way, I would take it. But for me to live, you must die. I have been in an unending nightmare since my death. Your soul is pure. You will continue on to the beyond.*

Since her death? Iris had an idea. She had to let Crina take over for it to work. The floating sensation took over Iris as she let go, drifting into Crina's memories.

The candles fluttered as Dena opened the door. "How's it going in here?" she asked.

Crina kept her eyes forward, but her peripheral vision was on the door.

"Everyone's gone," Dena was saying. "Lauren and Carys are busy cleaning up. I figured the less people around, the less chance of more casualties."

"Way to sugarcoat things," Wade said.

She clapped his back on the way to Violet. "Just keeping it real."

As Crina passed the table by Miri, her hand brushed against the wood, and a thought sparked. She flipped over the table, the candles falling off the top hitting the floor. The flames caught the flaps at the bottom of the nearby couch on fire.

"Get water," Miri said as she stomped on the other candles to put them out.

Crina darted for the door, swung it open, and sprinted across the driveway. Her head hurt as her feet pounded on the pavement. She could hear boots thudding behind her but she didn't look back. Iris had to die. That was it. She had to go away for Crina to fully take control and own her body.

"Crina, stop!" Wade yelled.

She kept running, not daring to stop. The neighborhood houses were dark. Hardly any lights were on. The shell of pumpkins with their carved faces stared at her from the porches, bringing memories back to her.

The faces.

Disapproving and full of hate.

She pushed harder, picking up speed. The air rushing in burned her throat and a pain stabbed at her side.

The faces.

Her parents.

Her brothers.

Sisters.

Full of concern.

The villagers.

Judging and full of hate.

Do you remember them? Iris asked. With each memory she released of Crina's, Iris grew stronger. Iris found one image she believed would stop Crina.

His face.

Armand.

Crina had thought he loved her. He said he did. She believed him, or she wouldn't have given herself to him, much less several times. They'd meet in the meadow, heat between them building with each touch. After they made love, they lay in the meadow on her mother's patchwork blanket. Picked flowers and teased each other.

The faces.

Knowing and hateful.

Iris flipped through the images, concentrating on the ones she thought would hurt the most.

Again, her sister's face. Mother. Father.

They knew what Crina had done. Performing acts that only a married woman was allowed to do. She was his wife, if not by ceremony but by actions. He betrayed her. Destroyed her.

Tomas. He wanted to help her. Marry her. Make a family for her daughter.

Oana. Small and helpless, with strawberry-blond curls. Her pudgy hand grabbing Crina's finger. The murky river.

Water burning her throat. The last words she heard from Armand just before she went under: "Crina! Please. I am sorry. I truly loved...*love* you."

No. Stop, Crina pleaded.

I forgive you, Iris thought.

Crina stopped. The tears were hot on her cheeks. Was Iris causing them or was she? The emotions inside her were boggled. She couldn't tell which were hers. A memory of Iris and Violet hit her. They were young with strawberry-blond pigtails, laughing and running on the beach with an older man struggling in the sand to keep up with them.

I am destroying Iris.

Her face.

Iris's face. Kind and gentle the first time Crina saw it in the mirror.

She covered that face with her hands and cried.

Wade, strong but caring. He loved Iris.

Just as Crina had loved Armand.

The faces.

The footsteps behind her slowed. "Iris?"

Wade.

Iris turned. She was back. A rush of air brushed her face, cooling the tears on her cheeks. The faces. Iris's family and friends. Full of love and caring.

"It's me," she said to him. "Let's get rid of Crina."

Wade came to her side and slipped his hand in hers. It was warm, comforting, as they walked in silence back to the apartment. The tears blurring her eyes made the streetlights look hazy.

The fire was out when they entered the apartment. A charred smell floated in the air.

Violet's face lit up. "Iris?"

Wade nodded.

"Shall we do this?" Iris released Wade's hand and stepped

into the middle of the circle.

Daisy stood from her seat at the tiny kitchenette table and hugged Iris. "Don't worry. I can do this."

"I know you can." Iris kissed her cheek.

Daisy let her go and took a seat on the floor in front of the circle. "I'm not sure how this works, but no matter what, don't leave the circle."

Iris smiled down at her. Daisy reminded Iris of the images she saw of Crina's little sisters. All five of them. They had hopeful eyes, just like Daisy's. But their eyes had wanted food to fill their hungry bellies. After each encounter with the Van Buren heir, Crina would bring home breads and meats to them. Sometimes even fruit. Armand was a generous lover, but he was also selfish. He broke Crina's heart to be a count.

Daisy chanted under her breath in the Romanian tongue of Crina's homeland.

Unbind the two souls intertwined. Release the spirit and send her home. Crina translated in her head. *You impress me, Iris, but you will not win.*

Daisy's hand hovered over a card. The Empress card. An image of an empress sitting on her throne, a crown of stars on her head, a staff in her hand, and a shield at her feet. It represented new birth.

A strong energy hit Iris and her control slipped. She tried to hold on to it, not give in, but the next hit sent her back.

Please don't do this. It was like she was sinking into a murky black pool, unable to move.

Crina knew each card. How could she not know them? She had been bound to them for centuries. When a fate changer takes her own life, her soul is trapped inside her tarot cards for eternity or until another fate changer released her. But because Crina sought revenge on Armand and his heirs, her hate turned her into the very thing she had created—the curse.

She hadn't known about her gift. Her mother hadn't known Crina had inherited the ability from her father. She came across her cards in the village. An old woman stopped her. Called her *Lemniscate* and handed her a deck. When she touched the cards, she claimed them. If she had known changing Armand's fate would have sealed hers, she wouldn't have done it. Fate changers are unable to change their own fates, or she would have. Instead, her anger and thirst for revenge brought her to kill herself.

Are you giving me these thoughts, Iris? Stop!

While Crina was distracted in the memories Iris was sending her, Iris pushed and pushed to gain control. A headache stabbed at her temples. Iris was almost out.

Crina glanced at the circle of cards, and Iris knew she would try to break the circle. She concentrated on her legs. *Stiff and heavy like concrete.*

Her legs shook as Crina tried to take a step but couldn't.

Stop it! Let me go. A panic rose in Crina's chest, and Iris had her. She pushed to take control, but Crina held on.

Wade, Violet, and Dena off to the side watched them with worried faces. Miri waved a lit bunch of herbs, sending smoke and a scent of sage across the room.

Don't send me back, Iris. Crina's voice was strained. *Please. I can't suffer it anymore.*

And I should suffer instead? Iris yelled and used all her force to push harder. *You're crazy. You already had your body. Your chance at life. You decided to end it. There's no do overs.*

"No, Daisy," Crina cried. "Don't touch that card. Please."

"I'm sorry. She's my sister." Daisy touched the card.

The empress on the card lit up and fluttered, then the others followed, creating a ripple until the final card settled into place. Images shot up from the cards, and Crina recognized them all.

Who are they? Iris felt stronger. Her fingers thawed like

frozen skin near a warm fire. The images were holograms of people from a long-ago past.

My family, Crina answered.

The faces.

Her parents, her sisters and brothers.

Grandparents, aunts, and uncles.

Oana.

The firstborn sons whose lives she'd stolen.

None judging.

None angered.

Only friendly smiles greeted her. Their eyes told her more than any words could. They forgave her. Just like Iris had. The hate left her heart, flying off like debris on the wind. A warmth rushed through her veins. It was a strange feeling. All she'd ever known was the cold.

Her mother reached out her arms and spoke in her soft, soothing voice. The language of her people warmed her soul. *It is time, dear one. Time for you to come home.*

Tingles and sparks rushed through Iris's body as Crina came out of it and turned. She was beautiful with long wavy hair and big doe eyes. Dressed in the memory of a peasant girl, she wore a skirt, blouse, and shawl.

Somewhere outside, a car door slammed shut, followed by another one.

Crina looked pointedly at Daisy. "You are strong, little flower. My departure won't end the curse. You must stop it. There is only one firstborn left. The curse lives in him. Find the new Armand. End the curse, and future firstborns will be safe."

Crina stepped into her mother's arms. The other spirits surrounded them, merging until they became one bright light, blinding Iris. The tarot cards shot up in the air and rained down around her.

There was no movement. Everyone was silent. The proof

that there was life after death stunned them all to their spots. Iris glanced around at the others. "Oh my gosh! Did you see that? Was it real?"

Wade nodded soundlessly.

"It was real," Violet said and hugged Dena.

"Of course it was." Miri started picking up the tarot cards, as if nothing spectacular had just happened.

Daisy shot up to her feet and embraced Iris. "We did it."

Iris hugged her back. "You did it, Daisy, and you were amazing."

Violet practically knocked her sisters down as she threw her arms around the two of them. "She's gone, right?"

Iris pulled back from her sisters, swaying. Her legs were weak and her hands were shaking. "Yes, it's me."

Wade caught her just as her legs gave way and held her in his strong arms. "I've got you."

She twisted to see his beautiful face. Concern crinkled around his deep brown eyes. "Don't ever let go."

"Never."

The door flew open, startling them all. Aster stormed in with Reese right behind her.

Chapter Twenty-Four

It was unusually warm for November. The ocean lifted and lowered the sailboat as it pushed through the waves. Iris sat on the deck, wearing jeans and a hoodie. Her face toward the sun, she sighed. Wade could watch her all day. Her every movement drove him nuts. He wanted her more than anything in the world, but he could be patient. She was worth the wait.

"This is pure heaven," she said and glanced over at him. "Do you not agree?"

Wade raised an eyebrow at her.

She pinched a look at him. "What?"

"You sounded like Crina."

"I did not." She straightened and swung her legs over the side. "Okay, maybe I did. Guess we got to know each other pretty well while sharing this body."

"Do you want mustard on your sandwich?" Violet called from the cabin.

"Yes," Wade said.

Dena and Violet were like a well-managed campaign as they made sandwiches in the small kitchen. Aster and Reese cuddled on the deck on the other side of Iris. Daisy lay on her back on the bow, her knees up as she read a book.

The events weighed on Wade's mind. Magic was real. Iris couldn't change fates but her sisters, Aster and Daisy, could. What did that mean? Could they make the world a better place for people? If they could, why wouldn't they want to do it?

"Have you thought about your gift?" he asked, looking at Aster.

"I think about it all the time," she said, taking a sip from her water bottle. "Why do you ask?"

"You could help people." He turned the wheel slightly.

"It comes with a price," Violet said, coming up the steps holding two sandwiches wrapped in paper towels.

"No, it doesn't," Aster said, taking the sandwich Violet offered her. "I figured a way to filter it."

"Then why not?" Wade noticed the frown on Iris's face. "What? You think she shouldn't."

Iris pushed loose hair behind her ear. "I got a lot of stuff from Crina's thoughts. They used crystals and stones as filters while fate changing. Doing that did prevent bad fates from going to the fate changer's family, but it has to go somewhere. It ends up inside the changer. Ages their insides. Some bled to death. Many didn't make it to twenty-five. It's a painful way to die."

"That sounds bad," Wade said. "Why did they change them?"

"They didn't know. Crina discovered it after her death," Iris said.

"Fates aren't supposed to be changed," Reese said. "The decisions we make direct our fates. People need to make the right choices in their life and not be careless with them."

"You're so right." Aster smiled and kissed him. "I'm glad you're my choice."

"Why are we all so serious?" Dena stomped up to the deck, two more sandwiches in her hand. "We are young. What's that song... Anyway, we should celebrate. I say we forget this crazy stuff and let loose."

"Yeah, we should address the elephant in the room... um...boat. I can't believe you two are engaged," Iris said, glancing over at Aster and Reese.

"It's a long engagement," she said and looked down at the big rock on her finger. "I'll be twenty-one by then."

Reese rubbed her back. "We aged years after what we went through. I believe we can handle anything together."

Wade smiled at Iris and she gave him one back. He understood what Reese meant. He'd weathered a storm with Iris. Almost losing her had put everything in perspective for him. It would have crushed him, and he couldn't imagine his life without her in it. His best friend. There was no one else for him but Iris. No matter how cliché it sounded, she completed him.

He faced forward, watching the bow jump waves as he steered. Iris came up behind him and wrapped her arms around his waist, leaning her head against him. He twisted to bring her to his side, his arm sliding down her back until his hand rested on her hip. Their bodies fitted together like two puzzle pieces. His heart felt at home with her.

The boat rocked, and he held her tighter so she wouldn't lose her footing. She tilted her head, and he kissed her soft lips. Her hand traveled up his chest and behind his neck, slender fingers combing through his hair. Lips parting, her tongue found his, sending a shiver down his spine. He wanted to get lost in her.

She pulled away from him, and, balancing on her toes, she whispered in his ear, "We're going to make it, too."

He smiled down at her. "I'd bet the boat on it."

Acknowledgments

I had such a fun time writing this book. While creating it, I pulled from many relationships in my own life. Iris and Wade's relationship is one that grew from a friendship much like mine and my husband's had. The connection Iris has to her sisters, I have with my own sister and best friend, Paula Ashmore. We've shared millions of wonderful moments together. I'm grateful to have such tight bonds. Also, I'm lucky to have many others who have helped to get this book published.

A huge thank you to my publisher and editor, Liz Pelletier, for believing in my stories and me. The fates knew what they were doing when they sent you into my life. Did I say thank you? Because once is just not enough. Thank you, thank you, thank you from the bottom of my heart.

A sincere thank you to Stacy Abrams for touching this story with her editing magic. From your talent to the care you take in your work, you are simply the best.

To my agent, Peter Knapp, thank you for always watching out for me. With each book, I remember that dark moment before you entered my life and changed my career. You're the best!

Immense gratitude to the entire Entangled Publishing team that worked on this book from editing to cover design to marketing and everything I'm forgetting to mention. Thank you for making my books pretty and getting them into readers' hands.

Thank you to the wonderful Jami Nord for giving such a wonderful critique of this book. You are amazing! To Pintip Dunn for pushing me to finish when I was just too tired to keep going. Love you! To Heather Cashman for the many phone calls of encouragement and for assisting me in my contests so I could get my writing done. To Nikki Roberti for also helping with the contests and for making me smile often.

To my writer friends here in Albuquerque who meet for coffee whenever we can (we miss you Veronica Bartles), to the wonderful Pitch Wars community, and my online friends, thank you for keeping me company and just for being genuinely awesome.

Thank to my family and friends for being so supportive and reminding me each day what really matters. And mostly, to my wonderful husband, Richard Drake, who supports me in all the ways so I can do this thing I love.

And finally, to you, dear reader, thank you for reading Iris and Wade's story. I hope you enjoy it as much as I enjoyed writing it.

About the Author

Brenda Drake grew up the youngest of three children, an Air Force brat, and the continual new kid at school. Her fondest memories growing up is of her eccentric, Irish grandmother's animated tales, which gave her a strong love for storytelling. So it was only fitting that she would choose to write stories with a bend toward the fantastical. When she's not writing or hanging out with her family, she haunts libraries, bookstores, and coffee shops, or reads someplace quiet and not at all exotic (much to her disappointment).

Made in the USA
Charleston, SC
15 March 2017